"For when the One Great Scorer
comes to write against your name,
he marks—not that you won or lost—but
*how* you played the game."

**—Grantland Rice**

★ ★ ★ ★ ★ ★

"Grantland Rice, the great sportswriter,
once said, 'It's not whether you win or
lose, it's how you play the game.' Well,
Grantland Rice can go to hell
as far as I'm concerned."

**—Gene Autrey**

★ ★ ★ ★ ★ ★

"Winning isn't everything …
it's **THE ONLY THING!**"

**—Vince Lombardi**

# THE ONLY THING

A contemporary historical novel inspired by actual events

*Written by* Dave Horning

*Illustrated by* Mark Sean Wilson

*Edited by* Limus Woods

*The Only Thing*
By Dave Horning
Edited by Limus Woods
Illustrations by Mark Sean Wilson

Field of Play Press
PO Box 1555
Hilliard, OH 43026

## Disclaimer:
**Anyone under the age of 18 should only wrestle when there is adult supervision. All wrestlers should wear headgear for the protection of the ears. Let's stay safe!**

Editor: Limus Woods
Illustrations: Mark Sean Wilson
Book design: Kendra Cagle
eBook design: Jetlaunch.net

Editorial: Inspira Literary Solutions

Library of Congress Control Number: 2021948813

ISBN:  978-1-7369592-0-6 (paperback)
       978-1-7369592-1-3 (Kindle)
       978-1-7369592-2-0 (ePub)

# TABLE OF CONTENTS

★ ★ ★　★ ★ ★

Prologue . . . . . . . . . . . . . . . . . . . . . . . . . . . . . . . . . . . . . . . . . . . . . . . . . . . . . . . i
Preface . . . . . . . . . . . . . . . . . . . . . . . . . . . . . . . . . . . . . . . . . . . . . . . . . . . . . . . . iii
List of Characters . . . . . . . . . . . . . . . . . . . . . . . . . . . . . . . . . . . . . . . . . . . . . . . . x

## DAY 1
### Saturday, February 21, 1971

**Chapter 1:** Lennie Takes Center Stage . . . . . . . . . . . . . . . . . . . . . . . . . . . . . . . 3
*COAC Wrestling Tournament, Reynoldsburg High School, Reynoldsburg, Ohio*
　　　*Historical Snapshot 1-2 – Columbus, Ohio in February of 1971* . . . . . . . . . 14

**Chapter 2:** Jackie James Takes Charge . . . . . . . . . . . . . . . . . . . . . . . . . . . . . . . 17
*Metro League Wrestling Tournament, Columbus East High School, Columbus, Ohio*
　　　*Historical Snapshot 2-3 – The History of OSU and Buckeye Football* . . . . . . 27

**Chapter 3:** Jackie Brings It Home . . . . . . . . . . . . . . . . . . . . . . . . . . . . . . . . . . . 29
*James Family Home in Clintonville, Columbus, Ohio*
　　　*Historical Snapshot 3-4 – The History of Columbus Water* . . . . . . . . . . . . . . 35

## DAY 2
### Friday, February 26, 1971

**Chapter 4:** The Last Full Practice . . . . . . . . . . . . . . . . . . . . . . . . . . . . . . . . . . . 39
*Worthington Monroe High School, Columbus, Ohio*
　　　*Historical Snapshot 4-5 – Enveloping Events in Sports and Politics* . . . . . . . 52

**Chapter 5:** Jackie Meets Woody . . . . . . . . . . . . . . . . . . . . . . . . . . . . . . . . . . . . 55
*Columbus Clintonville High School, Columbus, Ohio*
　　　*Historical Snapshot 5-6 – Enveloping Events in Columbus* . . . . . . . . . . . . . . 63

# DAY 3
## Saturday, February 27, 1971

**Chapter 6:** The Fathers' Advice . . . . . . . . . . . . . . . . . . . . . . . . . . . . . . . . . . 69
  *Historical Snapshot 6-7 – Enveloping Events in Vietnam* . . . . . . . . . . . . . . 80

**Chapter 7:** Maverick Motivations . . . . . . . . . . . . . . . . . . . . . . . . . . . . . . . 83
  *Historical Snapshot 7-8 – The Columbus Public School System* . . . . . . . . . . 95

**Chapter 8:** Rick McCoy Startles His Son . . . . . . . . . . . . . . . . . . . . . . . . . . . 97
*In the Lobby at Broadleaf High School, Columbus, Ohio*

## The Ohio High School Interscholastic Federation (OHSIF) Central District Sectional Wrestling Tournament
*Broadleaf High School Gymnasium, Columbus, Ohio*

# FIRST-ROUND MATCHES

**Chapter 9:**   The 98-Pound Weakling . . . . . . . . . . . . . . . . . . . . . . . . . . . . 105

**Chapter 10:**   Can Gary Get His Act Together? . . . . . . . . . . . . . . . . . . . . . . . 113

**Chapter 11:**   Gino Lands a Fish . . . . . . . . . . . . . . . . . . . . . . . . . . . . . . . . 125

**Chapter 12:**   The Gorgeous George Show . . . . . . . . . . . . . . . . . . . . . . . . . 133

**Chapter 13:**   The Brothers . . . . . . . . . . . . . . . . . . . . . . . . . . . . . . . . . . . 139

**Chapter 14:**   Carlo Pays the Piper . . . . . . . . . . . . . . . . . . . . . . . . . . . . . . 151

**Chapter 15:**   Terry Duke's Firm Favorites . . . . . . . . . . . . . . . . . . . . . . . . . 161

**Chapter 16:**   Nic's Bad Decision . . . . . . . . . . . . . . . . . . . . . . . . . . . . . . . 169

**Chapter 17:**   The Main Event, The First and Second Periods . . . . . . . . . . . . . . 181

**Chapter 18:**   The Main Event, The Final Period . . . . . . . . . . . . . . . . . . . . . . 189

**Chapter 19:**   The Unexpected Conversation . . . . . . . . . . . . . . . . . . . . . . . . 203

**Chapter 20:**   The Only Thing That Matters . . . . . . . . . . . . . . . . . . . . . . . . . 211

To All Those in the Arena. . . . . . . . . . . . . . . . . . . . . . . . . . . . . . . . . . . . . . . . . . . .219

To All Those Who Make States . . . . . . . . . . . . . . . . . . . . . . . . . . . . . . . . . . . . . . .221

Afterword . . . . . . . . . . . . . . . . . . . . . . . . . . . . . . . . . . . . . . . . . . . . . . . . . . . . . . .223

The Golden Rule Poster . . . . . . . . . . . . . . . . . . . . . . . . . . . . . . . . . . . . . . . . . . . .226

Acknowledgments . . . . . . . . . . . . . . . . . . . . . . . . . . . . . . . . . . . . . . . . . . . . . . . . .227

About the Author, Illustrator and Editor . . . . . . . . . . . . . . . . . . . . . . . . . . . . . . .229

Endnotes . . . . . . . . . . . . . . . . . . . . . . . . . . . . . . . . . . . . . . . . . . . . . . . . . . . . . . . .231

Recommended Reading . . . . . . . . . . . . . . . . . . . . . . . . . . . . . . . . . . . . . . . . . . . . .239

Book Club Questions. . . . . . . . . . . . . . . . . . . . . . . . . . . . . . . . . . . . . . . . . . . . . . .241

An Overview of the Sport of Folkstyle Wrestling in 1970-71 . . . . . . . . . . . . . . . . . . .243

# ★ ★ ★ PROLOGUE ★ ★ ★

**W**ITH THE SCORE tied at 9, and only 26 seconds left, will Bobby McCoy complete his escape and take the lead, or will Jackie James put Bobby on his back and seal the victory?

For both teenagers, winning this high school wrestling match is crucial. Bobby needs the victory to show his demanding father that he is tough, and thereby secure his future; Jackie needs to impress the college football coaches in the stands that he is a winner who deserves a full-ride athletic scholarship.

The stakes could not be higher for either Bobby or Jackie. Will they do whatever it takes to win? At this moment, winning is…**THE ONLY THING**…that matters.

But after the match, an unexpected conversation changes everything.

Join Bobby, his teammates, and Jackie as they navigate their way through life in February of 1971 in Columbus Ohio. Against a backdrop of enveloping historical events, including the Vietnam draft, school segregation, and other issues of the day, they discover the only thing that really matters.

*A Contemporary Historical Novel*

# ★ ★ ★ PREFACE ★ ★ ★

THIS BOOK IS a work of contemporary historical fiction that I hope all readers (not just sports fans) will enjoy. Ultimately, this is a story about teenagers coming of age while participating in high school wrestling tournaments held one week apart.

One of the purposes of this book is to promote the sport of "folkstyle wrestling," the name for the type of wrestling commonly found in American high schools and colleges. I encourage you to attend an upcoming wrestling match, especially if you have a friend or family member who wrestles. As they said in the 1971 Alka-Seltzer commercial, "Try it! You'll like it!"

Between some chapters, I have provided historical information about the enveloping events of the day. I call them "Historical Snapshots." Consider each of them as an intermission during a movie. Some readers will skip over them, and some will find them interesting. The choice is yours.

The novel is set in Columbus, Ohio in February of 1971, two years and ten months after the assassination of Dr Martin Luther King, Jr. and just two years and eight months before the 1973 oil crisis, which changed America and the world forever.

## In February of 1971, there were many crosscurrents of conflict:

- Anti-war protesters versus those who still believed the Vietnam War could be won
- Union workers versus nonunion workers
- The ideals of Dr. Martin Luther King, Jr. versus the status quo

As the rules for folkstyle wrestling are not well-known, I have provided below the basic rules for Ohio high schools in 1970-71:

# Periods

- three periods – each two minutes
- the first period starts with both wrestlers standing on their feet
- for the next two periods, one starts in the up position and one in the down position

# Points

- two points for a takedown, one point for an escape, and two points for a reversal
- close counts – coming close to pinning your opponent earns two points (a "predicament"); coming really, really close earns three points (a "near fall").
- wrestlers can earn riding time advantage points – one for 60 to 119 seconds, and two for 120+ seconds of advantage (advantage over your opponent's amount of riding time).
- points can be awarded to a wrestler if their opponent stalls or uses dangerous holds. First, there is a warning. If the opponent continues to misbehave, then the referee will award one point, then another point, then two points, and then disqualification.

# Pins (aka Falls)

- regardless of the score, if one wrestler holds the other's shoulders to the mat for two seconds, they will win instant victory with a pin (aka "fall"). The match is over.

# Key Starting Positions

In the first period, both wrestlers start in the **Neutral Position**, which means that they are both on their feet.

This position is called the **Referee's Position**. The wrestler in the darker uniform is in the "up referee's position" or "up position." The wrestler on all fours is in the "down referee's position," or "down position." If a wrestler starts the second period in the up position, then that wrestler will start the third period in the down position.

It is also helpful to know that during a match, one wrestler will wear a green ankle band, and one will wear red. The scoreboard will always have the green score on the left, so the score will always be displayed with the green score first. A score of 3 – 7 means that the red wrestler is ahead by four points.

A more detailed overview (but not the complete rulebook!) of the rules that existed in 1970-71 can be found at the end of the book for those who want a more detailed explanation. Look for *"An Overview of the Rules of Folkstyle Wrestling in 1970-71."*

Since 2004, the Olympics has included women in freestyle wrestling, which is similar to but not exactly the same as folkstyle wrestling. In the 2016 Rio de Janeiro Olympics, American Helen Maroulis won the Gold Medal in the 53 kg (116.6 lbs) weight class. American J'den Cox won a Bronze Medal at the 86 kg (189.2 lbs) weight class in the men's division.

In the 2020 Tokyo Olympics (held in July and August of 2021), the American team's performance in freestyle wrestling was outstanding, winning nine medals in the twelve weight classes contested. That was more than any other nation!

## Here are the medal winners:

- **GOLD** – Tamyra Mensah, 68 kg (149.6 lbs), women's freestyle
- **GOLD** – David Taylor, 86 kg (189.2 lbs), men's freestyle
- **GOLD** – Gable Steveson, 125 kg (275 lbs), men's freestyle
- **SILVER** – Adelaine Gray, 76 kg (167.2 lbs), women's freestyle
- **SILVER** – Kyle Snyder, 97 kg (213.4 lbs), men's freestyle
- **BRONZE** – Sarah Hildebrandt, 50 kg (110 lbs), women's freestyle
- **BRONZE** – Helen Maroulis, 57 kg (125.4 lbs), women's freestyle
- **BRONZE** – Thomas Gilman, 57kg (125.4 lbs), men's freestyle
- **BRONZE** – Kyle Dake (Yeah! Cornell Big Red!), 74 kg (162.8 lbs), men's freestyle

I have profound respect for all who wrestle. If "egalitarianism" is the political doctrine that holds that all people in a society should have equal rights and opportunities from birth,[1] then I consider wrestling to be the most egalitarian of all high school sports. Just you against a same-sized opponent, without a teammate, ball, or weapon. Neither status, nor privilege, nor popularity will matter. You give that all up when you step onto a wrestling mat.

I encourage all middle school and high school students who have an interest in wrestling to try out! A strong and fit body will be your participation trophy. Talk to your parents and the wrestling coach or athletic director at your school for more information. Step into the arena!

If you are already a wrestling fan and this is repetitious, I beg your patience as we introduce the sport we love to those unfamiliar.

—*Dave Horning*

# List of Characters:

## The Worthington Monroe Wrestling Team

- **Robert "Bobby" McCoy** – *175-pound weight class* – Junior – 17 years old

- **Gary "Hambone" Hamilton** – *105-pound weight class* – Senior, Co-Captain – 18 years old

- **Lawrence "Lonnie" Williams** – *98-pound weight class* – Sophomore – Lonnie and Gary wrestle each other frequently as practice partners.

- **Giovanni "Gino" Ciccolini** – *112-pound weight class* – Junior – Gino and Gary also wrestler each other frequently in practice. Gino is well-liked by many friends.

- **George "Gorgeous George" Bauchmire** – *119-pound weight class* – Sophomore – George is a natural athlete who is having surprising success in his first year on varsity.

- **Michael "Mikey" McKelvey** – *126-pound weight class* – Sophomore – Mike is the younger brother of Mark McKelvey, the 132-pounder.

- **Mark "Marky" McKelvey** – *132-pound weight class* – Junior, Co-Captain

- **Carlo "Rossi" Rossini** – *138-pound weight class* – Junior – Carlo has great natural talent and could be a state qualifier if he could only develop the discipline to give up drinking and smoking…and partying…and staying out late…

- **Wayne "Flex" Fleckman** – *145-pound weight class* – Junior – Wayne is double-jointed and is therefore very flexible, which provides a unique advantage.

- **Bruce "Bulldog" Landers** – *155-pound weight class* – Sophomore – Bulldog's main passion is football, so he does not cut weight to wrestle in a lower weight class.

- **Dominic "Nic" Stavroff** – *167-pound weight class* – Senior – Nic plays high school football and intends to play football in college. Nic is a fan of the Green Bay Packers and Vince Lombardi. He embraces the ideal that winning is the only thing that matters.

- **Kendall "Kenny" Lambert** – *185-pound weight class* – Senior – For Kenny, winning is fun but losing a wrestling match would not cause him stress.

- **Leonard "Lennie" Coulton** – *Heavyweight weight class* – Junior – Lennie is a very large teenager, weighing 345 pounds. His physique is that of an out-of-shape and overweight person. But his appearance belies a tremendous muscular strength…and nimbleness. (In later years, the Ohio High School Interscholastic Federation (OHSIL) would impose a 285-pound weight limit.)

- **Sebastian "Sparky" Thompson** – *Team Manager* – Junior – Responsible for cleaning and taping the mats before each practice. Quirky, but extremely loyal and dedicated to his work, which is appreciated by all. Everyone considers Sparky an important part of the team.

- **Terry Duke** – *Worthington Monroe Mavericks High School Wrestling Coach* – A former football player and heavyweight wrestler in high school

- Lloyd Bennett – Worthington Monroe Mavericks Assistant Wrestling Coach

## The Worthington Monroe High School Community

- **Casandra "Cassie" Stimson** – *Bobby McCoy's girlfriend*, also a Worthington Monroe High School Junior. Cassie is a young woman with a sparkling personality who loves Bobby – 17 years old.

- **Richard "Rick" McCoy, Sr.** – *Bobby's father*. A member of the local plumber's union who holds prejudices against African Americans. He supports President Richard Nixon and the effort to win the Vietnam War.

- **Georgia McCoy** – *Bobby's mother*. She is a stay-at-home housewife, a common vocation before the 1973 oil crisis.

- **Richard "Dick" McCoy, Jr.** – *Bobby's older brother*, who died serving his country in the Vietnam War.

- **Ronald "Ron" McCoy** – *Bobby's uncle and Rick's brother*, a self-employed and nonunion electrical contractor who works in new home construction

- **Carl Hamilton** – *Gary's father*. Carl is the owner of a local distribution company. He also supports President Richard Nixon and the effort to win the Vietnam War.

## The Columbus Clintonville High School Wrestling Team

- **Jackie James** – *175-pound weight class* – Junior – 17 years old – Jackie is also a very good football player.

## The Columbus Clintonville High School Community

- **Edward "Ed" Lawson**– *Columbus Clintonville High School Football and Wrestling Coach.* He coaches Jackie James in both sports.

- **Lydia Flower** – *Columbus Clintonville High School Secretary to the Principal,* a mother of a Clintonville wrestler and a friend of Elizabeth James

- **Joshua James** – *Jackie's father.* He is a man of incredible strength, which allows him to handle the strenuous work at Buckeye Steel Castings, including over-time, and still have energy for a part-time job as a janitor at Columbus Clintonville High School. No one calls him "Josh."

- **Elizabeth Madison James** – *Joshua's wife and Jackie's mother.* Like her husband, Elizabeth is very religious and has raised all of her children to be people of faith.

- **Aaron James** – *Child #1* – Jackie's older brother. Aaron played halfback at Otterbein College, known today as Otterbein University

- **Jackie James** – *Child #2*

- **Samuel "Sam" James** – *Child #3* – 15 years old

- **Rachel James** – *Child #4* – Nine years old, the youngest child and the only girl

## Real Life Historical Figures

- **Woodrow "Woody" Hayes** – *the Head Coach for football at The Ohio State University* from 1951 to 1978

- **Rudy Hubbard** – *the Assistant Football Coach (for running backs) at The Ohio State University* from 1968 to 1973

**★ ★ ★ ★ ★ ★**

Saturday, February 20, 1971

# CHAPTER 1

★ ★ ★

## Lennie Takes Center Stage

......................................................................................................

### 1970-71 Central Ohio Athletic Conference
### High School Wrestling Tournament

Reynoldsburg High School
Reynoldsburg, Ohio
*Heavyweight Championship Match*

......................................................................................................

## Robert "Bobby" McCoy, Worthington Monroe 175-Pounder

**B**OBBY WHISTLED LOW and slow as he looked back and forth between the heavyweight rivals about to compete for their conference championship. The contrast was stark.

His teammate, Leonard "Lennie" Coulton, wrestled heavyweight for the Worthington Monroe Mavericks, and he was enormous. Three hundred and forty-five pounds! Lennie's upper torso, a blend of bone and muscle under rolls of fat, defied a regular uniform. His ragged, makeshift green jersey, with its shoulders cut off, didn't match the green sweatpants, embellished with a handsewn stripe, which covered his tree-trunk legs.

The crowd favorite was Lennie's opponent, a six-foot-two, trim and muscular 215-pound senior from Westland High School. Handsome, too. The seasoned athlete was showing comfort in the moment, looking calm and relaxed as he was warming up, obviously confident. And why not? He was an all-district linebacker with full-ride athletic scholarship offers from Notre Dame, Wisconsin, and Miami University of Ohio. Then, Bobby noticed the Westland linebacker clench his jaw and shake his head back and forth, clearly showing disdain for Lennie.

Bobby elbowed his teammate, Gary "Hambone" Hamilton, the Mavericks' 105-pounder, who was sitting in the stands next to him, and said, "Looks like Lennie is in for some stiff competition."

"Nah! Remember that underneath it all, Lennie's strong. It's his hidden advantage," Gary said.

Bobby remembered. Early in the season, Coach Terry Duke, the Maverick's head wrestling coach, had asked Bobby to practice with Lennie—so Bobby did. Once. *Felt like I was wrestling a bear,* Bobby recalled.

Lennie moved to his spot on the center circle, knelt down, and fastened the green ankle band just above his wrestling shoe. His opponent took the red one.

"Shake hands. Ready? Wrestle!" called the referee. The match was on.

At the start of the match, the Westland linebacker reached around Lennie's neck with his right hand, initiating a collar tie. Soon, both wrestlers were in the tie-up position.

Lennie also put his left hand behind his opponent's neck and pulled down. The Westland linebacker tried to break the tie-up by lowering his head into Lennie's chest and trying to push away—but that was a mistake.

Lennie then bore his weight down on top of the Red wrestler and they both fell flat to the mat. The crowd gasped. *Had Lennie crushed the life out of his rival?*

But Lennie fell so that most of his weight landed on his own knees. He pushed his toes into the mat to raise his knees off of it, forcing all of his weight onto his rival's back. He then tiptoed 180 degrees around his opponent, completing the go behind in three hops. The audience leaned back in their seats, dazzled by Lennie's unexpected agility.

The referee signaled two points for the takedown, and the Mavericks roared their approval. Bobby and most of Lennie's teammates, now dressed in their street clothes, had stayed to watch his championship match.

By the end of the match, the Westland linebacker's confident expression was gone. He breathed deeply to regain the energy he'd lost moving Lennie's enormous weight. The match was never in doubt; Lennie won 7 – 2.

"Huge win," yelled Coach Duke. "You just won the conference championship!"

Lennie had also won over the crowd. They were standing and giving a warm round of applause to both wrestlers.

Lennie's teammates cheered the loudest, whooping it up for their guy. Lennie had pulled through three times during the regular season when the outcome of a dual match (just one team against another) came down to the heavyweights. All three times, Lennie's win sealed the team victory. Now, hearing their support, he threw his hands skyward.

A cry rang out from the Westland crowd: "That's not fair!"

The Mavericks looked for the heckler.

The Westland whiner screamed, "There should be a limit on how much a heavyweight can weigh. It's not fair! Our guy never had a chance!"

"You're right," bellowed Carlo "Rossi" Rossini, the Mavericks' 138-pounder. "Your guy never had a chance!"

Gary, exercising his duties as a co-captain, elbowed Carlo. "Shut up, Rossi! Your mouth is gonna start a fight!"

Gary was right. The Mavericks eyed the Westland team, some shaking their fists. Carlo gulped and said, "Okay, okay, guys. Let's join Lennie on the mat! Now!"

The Mavericks climbed down from the stands and joined Lennie and Coach Duke on the center mat. The Westland crowd made for the exits.

Bobby led the cheers, shouting, "Way to go, Lennie!"

"Congratulations!" added Giovanni "Gino" Ciccolini, the Mavericks' 112-pounder.

"Thanks, guys. I really appreciate you staying for my match," Lennie replied.

"We wouldn't have missed it," Carlo insisted. "We didn't want Hambone to be our only conference champion. We would never have heard anything else!"

Gary smiled at being needled. He expected nothing less from his teammates. "No sense arguing when you're right," replied Gary. Even Lennie laughed.

"Lennie! Go shower and join us in the lobby. We'll wait for you," said Coach Duke. He turned his attention to the others. "And I want all of you to wait! We will leave as a team."

As the Maverick contingent moved into the lobby, Bobby exhaled sharply in relief, seeing that the Westland crowd had already left the building. The Maverick wrestlers and their families broke up into small groups and waited so Lennie and his parents didn't have to straggle out alone into an unfamiliar environment. Gary headed toward his girlfriend, Julia, who was talking with his mother. Bobby spied his own girlfriend, Cassie, and led her to a private corner.

Cassie pulled Bobby into her arms and gave him a big hug. She leaned back and broke it off when he stiffened in response.

"What's up?" she complained. "Aren't you glad to see me?"

"Yes, of course," Bobby replied. "I'm just feeling down, I guess. I got pinned in the first round. When I lose like that, everyone is staring at my face, and I've got nowhere to hide. Sometimes, I wonder if wrestling is worth it."

Cassie hugged Bobby again, gently this time. After a few seconds, she pushed away again and said, "Well, it's gotten you into shape." She punched his muscular abdomen with playful blows. "Isn't that worth it?"

"Yeah, that's what Dad wants…for me to get in shape and be tough. But he's not the one out there in front of a crowd getting pinned. I feel like I'm doing this all for him… that I have no say."

"Please don't start an argument with him tonight," Cassie pleaded. "You know his temper. You'll get grounded again and we won't be able to get White Castle sliders. Just think of me and how hard I giggled when I saw you in those green tights for the first time. You looked like Robin Hood!"

When she stood on her tiptoes and kissed him on the cheek, Bobby gave her the hug she desired. Meanwhile, Bobby's father, Rick McCoy, entered the lobby. Spotting Bobby and Cassie, he called out, "C'mon, Bobby! Cassie! Let's go."

"Dad…we're all waiting for Lennie to get showered. It should only be a few more minutes. Coach wants us to stay and show Lennie we're together. Like a team. You know, like you and the guys down at the union hall."

"Okay, I get it…and I'm sure Lennie needs that shower," said Rick, but the joke fell flat.

"Hey, there's Gary and his mom over there," Rick continued. "I wonder if his dad is here."

Rick left his son and Cassie and joined Gary's group. "Where's your dad, Gary? Is he here?"

"Yes. Last I saw him, he was on the other side of the lobby talking with Nic. I'm sure he'll be happy to see you," said Gary, rolling his eyes.

"Hey, what can I say? We enjoy giving each other a hard time," replied Rick as he turned and walked away.

Against the wall on the far side of the lobby, Gary's father, Carl Hamilton, was talking with Carlo and Dominic "Nic" Stavroff, the Maverick 167-pounder.

"So, can I or can I not get an athletic scholarship for playing football at a small college?" asked Nic, throwing his hands in the air.

"Not a full-ride scholarship," Carl answered. "But small colleges can give grants based on financial need…and special abilities that contribute to the campus experience. For example, if that college needs a drum major and you can twirl a baton, you'll get more grant and less loan. And grants don't need to be repaid."

"Don't need to be repaid?" exclaimed Nic. "Now we're talking!"

"Hey, Carl, how's it going" interjected Rick McCoy, joining the group. "Great to see you again."

"Well, well, well! Look what the cat dragged in," replied Carl, shaking his head. Carl and Rick were strong supporters of Maverick wrestling, President Nixon, and the war in Vietnam. But they disagreed about unions. Rick, a leader in the local plumbing union, loved to goad Carl about being a nonunion shop.

"Have you called my friend at the Teamsters yet?" asked Rick.

"Gee, I think I lost his number…again," quipped Carl. It had been a running gag between them since the day they met, but there was an edge to it. Carl's company sold plastic and steel plumbing supplies to union contractors that hired union plumbers like Rick, but also to nonunion plumbers who often worked for homebuilders. Carl, like his competitors, hired nonunion to keep costs low. Carl knew that, to thrive in America, you had to compete and win.

The group's conversation returned to Nic's desire to play college football, and they explored the pluses and minuses of various Ohio colleges. Rick didn't seem to pay attention; everyone knew he had other plans for Bobby. Carlo thought about learning to twirl a baton.

## Carlo Rossini, Worthington Monroe 138-Pounder

From the corner of his eye, Carlo saw his parents walk through the lobby's main entrance. As he peeled away from the group discussing football, a cold shiver went down his spine. He had finished in fourth place in today's conference tournament… after winning the 132-pound title the previous year as a sophomore. But since he'd moved up a weight class, he was having trouble competing. Even at the higher weight class, Carlo struggled to make weight. His diet of beer and cigarettes didn't help. His shoulders slumped as he anticipated another tongue-lashing from his father.

"Hello, Carlo!" said his mother, pleasantly. "I'm proud of you for winning points for the team."

While Carlo gave his mother a hug, his eyes darted to his father, Rocco Rossini, standing nearby with a blank expression on his face.

"Carlo," Rocco began, "your mother and I have decided I should no longer scold you about your wrestling. She believes it is up to you now. In two years, you will be out of the house and on your own. I won't be there every day to tell you to wake up, eat breakfast, go to work, and go to bed."

Rocco took a deep breath and awkwardly continued, "I love you, son…and I always will. But from now on, your wrestling is in your own hands." Rocco frowned and threw his hands up in the air.

Carlo's jaw dropped. He ran his hand through his hair and then across his face, searching for a response. Fortunately for Carlo, Lennie entered the lobby to an enthusiastic round of applause.

Coach Duke began, shouting, "I would like to announce that, with Lennie's win in the heavyweight final, our team score moved ahead of Reynoldsburg's into third place. This is our best team finish yet in the conference. Congratulations to all of you. I appreciate all your hard work."

"Speech, Lennie! Speech!" came the cries from Gary and his co-captain Mark "Marky" McKelvey, the Mavericks' 132-pounder.

Before any words came out, Lennie's eyes went soft and tears welled in their corners. Thrusting a fist in the air, he hugged the team manager, Sebastian "Sparky" Thompson, and began: "Thanks, Coach, guys, friends, Mom and Dad. I think y'all know that before I joined the wrestling team last year, I was almost invisible at school. Pretty ironic for a big guy like me to be invisible, right?

"But being a part of this team…I have friends, my name is announced over the PA in homeroom, and people no longer look the other way when I walk down the hall. Heck, I even had a cheerleader wish me luck yesterday! You guys, all of you…my appreciation. Here's to Maverick wrestling!"

Lennie's mother wiped away her own tears.

"Hurray for Lennie! Hurray for Maverick wrestling!" shouted Sparky.

"Team! Team! Team!" came the shouts from his Maverick teammates.

## Gary "Hambone" Hamilton, Worthington Monroe 105-Pounder

The crowd broke up into family units and began exiting the lobby. Cassie and Bobby joined his father, Rick, still pestering Carl Hamilton. As the crowd thinned, Gary, his mother, and his girlfriend, Julia, also joined, forming one large group in the center of the lobby.

"Congratulations, son, on winning the 105-pound weight class." said Carl Hamilton. "We have a surprise for you. Your mom and I drove separately, so you can take your mom's car. Take Julia out for dinner, then give her a ride home."

With that, Carl Hamilton tossed the car keys to his son.

"That sounds good to me!" Gary said, smiling at Julia as he deftly caught the keys with one hand. "I am pretty hungry."

"Just don't stay out too late," Carl stipulated.

"Dad, I'm never late! Last Saturday, I was home at a quarter of twelve."

"A quarter of twelve?" Carl protested, "I was up past midnight, and you still were out!"

"Dad, I was home at three a.m., and three is exactly a quarter of twelve!"

Carl massaged his forehead while shaking it back and forth. Cassie and Julia giggled. Bobby looked at his father and received a glare in return. Bobby knew he could never joke around with his father like that. Bobby nodded, signaling that he got the message.

"Get out of here" Carl growled, "before I take those keys back!"

## Historical Snapshot 1-2:

......................................................................................

### Columbus, Ohio in February of 1971

- *The growth rate for the national economy was 3.3%.[2]*

- *The national unemployment rate was 6.0%.[2]*

- *Inflation was 4.3%.[3]*

- *Dow Jones was in the middle of a strong bull run, from a low of 631 on May 26, 1970 to 882 on February 25, 1971, an increase of 39% in less than a year. The bull run would continue and take the Dow Jones to over 1,000 in November of 1972 and peak at 1040 in early 1973 before falling all the way down to 577 in December 1974 because of the 1973 oil crisis.[4]*

- *In 1971, the average price for a gallon of gasoline in the USA was 36 cents. It would rise to 53 cents in 1974 and 86 cents by 1979.[5]*

- *The median income of the nation's families went above $10,000 in 1971 for the first time in U.S. history. The 1971 median family income of $10,290 was about 4 percent higher than the 1970 median of $9,870. However, because of price increases, the 1971 median income was slightly less than the 1970 median income in constant dollars.[6]*

- *In February 1971, the U.S. minimum wage was raised to $1.60, up from $1.45 the year before. This is equivalent to $10.33 in 2020 dollars.[7]*

- *The median price for a home in Columbus, Ohio was $16,000 in 1971, up from $15,500 in 1970. The median price for a home in Worthington, Ohio was $26,800 in 1971, up from $25,800 in 1970.[8]*

- *In 1971, when Freddie Mac began surveying lenders for mortgage data, interest rates for 20-year fixed-rate mortgages ranged from 7.29% to 7.73%.[9]*

- *A Columbus home buyer who put 20% down on a home valued at $16,000 would have a monthly mortgage payment of $103.12, assuming a 7.5% interest rate and a 20-year amortization.*

- *A Worthington home buyer who put 20% down on a home valued at $26,800 would have a monthly mortgage payment of $172.73, assuming a 7.5% interest rate and a 20-year amortization.*

- *A first-class postage stamp was six cents. It increased to eight cents in May 1971, another sign of the "creeping inflation" that existed in the early 1970s.[10]*

- *Monday Night Football began on September 21, 1970.*

- *Beginning on January 1, 1971, cigarette advertising was banned on TV and radio.*

- *In March 1971, both houses of the U.S. Congress passed a proposed constitutional amendment lowering the voting age to 18. The states ratified it four months later.*

- *In April 1971, the Oscar for Best Movie of 1970 went to* Patton, *and the Best Actor award went to George C. Scott, who played General Patton in that movie.*

- *For the week of February 21-27, 1971, the Billboard Hot 100 showed:*

- *#1 – "One Bad Apple" by The Osmonds[11]*

- *#2 – "Mama's Pearl" by The Jackson 5[11]*

- *For the same week, the Billboard R&B Hot 100 showed "Mama's Pearl" as #1.[12]*

- *The TV show,* All in the Family, *debuted on January 12, 1971. It quickly became the #1 TV show in America. The #2 show was* The Flip Wilson Show.[13]

- Car & Driver *magazine's list of Top 10 Cars for 1970 included the Dodge Charger and the Datsun 240Z.[14] The 1970 Chrysler New Yorker featured ventless front windows for the first time ever.[15]*

- *In 1971, a hamburger at McDonalds cost 21 cents, up from 20 cents in 1970. A Burger King Whopper cost 45 cents, a White Castle slider cost 15 cents, and a Wendy's Single cost 55 cents.[16]*

# CHAPTER 2

### ★ ★ ★

## Jackie James Takes Charge

. . . . . . . . . . . . . . . . . . . . . . . . . . . . . . . . . . . . . . . . . . . . . . . . . . . . . . . . . . . . . . . . . . . . . . . . . . . . . . . . . . . .

**1970-71 Metro League High School Wrestling Tournament**

Columbus East High School
Columbus, Ohio
*175-Pound Championship Match*

. . . . . . . . . . . . . . . . . . . . . . . . . . . . . . . . . . . . . . . . . . . . . . . . . . . . . . . . . . . . . . . . . . . . . . . . . . . . . . . . . . . .

## Jackie James, Columbus Clintonville 175-Pounder

**O**N EVERY THIRD Saturday in February, the Ohio High School Interscholastic Federation (OHSIF) mandates that all Ohio high school athletic conferences conduct their conference (league) championship tournaments for wrestling. Tonight, all over Ohio, conference championships were being conducted to determine the individual conference champions in each weight class and the overall team league champion. While the Columbus suburban high schools were gathered in Reynoldsburg for the Central Ohio Athletic Conference tournament, the high schools that were part of the Columbus Public School System were gathered close to downtown Columbus for the Metro League tournament.

After the 167-pound weight class championship match was completed and the winner announced, the rivals for the 175-pound weight class and their coaches took their places in opposite corners of the wrestling mat placed squarely in the center of the gymnasium. The crowd buzzed with anticipation, for these next two wrestlers were well-known high school football players also, both earning all-conference honors in the fall. Bill Nettles smoothed back his shaggy blond hair in preparation for putting on his wrestling headgear. He removed his sky blue warm-up jacket to reveal a trim, athletic body with not an ounce of fat. Jackie James put on his headgear over his medium afro. He was noticeably shorter. It looked to be a potential disadvantage until he removed his dark red warm-up jacket and revealed a bodybuilder's physique.

Receiving the go-ahead signal from the referee, the public address announcer introduced the next match: "And now, for the 175-Pound Championship Match. Jackie James of Clintonville High School versus Bill Nettles of Walnut Ridge High School."

Jackie and Bill had been Metro League rivals in a wrestling match a year earlier when they were sophomores, and in a football game the previous fall when they were juniors. They each had one win. Jackie's team won the football game, but Bill won the wrestling match when they were sophomores. This would be the decider.

They jumped up and down in their respective corners to loosen their muscles. There would be no stare down between these familiar combatants. Neither seasoned athlete could be intimidated. Now, it was now all about heart—the desire to win.

"Jackie!" pleaded his coach, "No finesse moves out there tonight, okay? This guy's too strong for that, unless the move is executed perfectly. He can create offense from a defensive position. Be careful! Keep your knees away from your head so you don't get cradled like last year. Get ready for a lot of hand fighting and tie-ups." Jackie nodded, still bouncing on the mat.

"Wrestlers! Take your ankle bands," called the referee. Jackie's uniform was bold red, so he grabbed the red ankle band. That left the green one for Bill, on the left, wearing sky blue.

"Shake hands. Ready? Wrestle!" called the referee.

Jackie and Bill sidestepped in a circle, hand fighting, grabbing, pulling, and shoving. Each wrestler was looking for an opening to lunge forward and "shoot" for a takedown.

After Bill put his right hand behind Jackie's neck in a collar tie, they were soon in the classic tie-up position.

Bill gained an advantageous hold, but Jackie pushed away and out of the tie-up.

They pushed and pulled each other, still looking for an opening. They tied up and broke it off twice. Then, Bill grabbed Jackie's neck with a collar tie, and pulled down.

When Jackie resisted, his head came up and Bill lunged forward, shooting for a single leg sweep.

Bill had forged beyond Jackie's initial defense!

Jackie adapted to the challenge. As Bill stepped forward with his right leg to finish the takedown, Jackie inserted a whizzer with his left arm.

Jackie laid the weight of his torso into Bill's shoulder, driving him down to the mat. No wrestler wants to be forced onto their back, so Bill let his right arm go limp, enabling him to pull it off Jackie's back. Bill dove in the direction Jackie was pushing, his newly freed right arm by his side. Bill landed on his stomach and Jackie landed on top of him.

The crash of both bodies onto the mat brought Jackie's supporters to their feet. The closed-cell foam mat cushioned their fall so the wrestlers felt no pain.

"Two points, Red! Takedown!" called the referee. Since the green lights were on the left side of the tabletop scoreboard at the scorer's table, and the red lights were on the right, the scoreboard displayed the score as 0 – 2.

Bill was soon on all fours and, leaning back into Jackie, he raised his left leg off the mat and planted his foot firmly. Continuing to lean back, Bill brought his right leg up, blocked Jackie's right arm from reaching around his waist, got hip separation, and finished the stand-up escape.

"One point, Green! Escape!" called the referee, competing against the crowd noise. Encouragement was coming from both sides.

*Phweet!* The referee's whistle blew. "First period over!" called the referee. The score was Bill 1 – Jackie 2.

The referee motioned the wrestlers to the center of the mat for the coin toss to decide who would be up and who would be down. Bill won the coin toss and gave the referee a "thumbs up." Jackie took the down referee's position for the start of the second period.

*Phweet!*

Jackie leaned back into Bill and brought his left knee forward for the stand-up. Jackie almost got to his feet, but Bill reached around Jackie's waist and then drove his right shoulder into Jackie's back, returning Jackie to the mat.

Bill was not strong enough to keep Jackie flat on the mat, but he kept control. Bill maintained his strong ride by holding onto Jackie's left ankle, blocking any future stand-up attempts. Bill might have thought about going legs-in, but he must have decided Jackie was too strong.

Eventually, Jackie got to all fours and started the outside switch move. Bill tried to hold onto Jackie's left arm, but Jackie flexed his bicep and broke Bill's grip.

Jackie drove his right elbow hard into Bill's upper torso. No finesse indeed!

The hard elbow gave Jackie the separation he needed to scissor his own legs and reach in between Bill's.

Jackie drove his right shoulder into Bill's torso and cut the corner to finish the reversal.

"Two points! Red! Reversal!" The score was Bill 1 – Jackie 4.

Bill was able to escape again just before the period ended. After two periods, Jackie was leading 2–4.

Before the start of the third period, Jackie caught the eye of his coach, Coach Ed Lawson, and walked over—a signal that he was open to guidance. Coach Lawson didn't disappoint. "Use the arm chop. Keep him on the mat. If he gets to his knees, he gets to his feet."

At the whistle, Jackie's ferocious arm chop worked. Bill was a table with one leg missing. Jackie put his weight on Bill's back and drove him to the mat.

Jackie was a monster on top. He gave Bill a tough ride, using his upper body and arm strength to fight Bill's efforts to get to all fours. It worked for the first half of the third period.

Bill put it all together for one last best effort. He rose to all fours, the starting point for his go-to move. And why not the same move? Bill's left leg was stronger than Jackie's left arm, and it always would be!

Bill pulled Jackie's wrist away from his waist and broke free.

"One point! Green! Escape!" called the referee. The score was Bill 3 – Jackie 4. Bill only needed a takedown to come from behind and win.

Jackie and Bill resumed their sidestepping dance with reduced hand fighting, focusing instead on huffing and puffing to catch oxygen. Which one would be able to execute when fatigued? Which wrestler had heart?

Bill found an opening and lunged at both of Jackie's legs, shooting for a double leg takedown.

Jackie threw his legs back in the air to counter Bill's shoot, but Bill had a strong grip. Bill crawled forward on his knees, gaining better control of Jackie's hips with each advance. Jackie countered by hopping backwards to keep his weight on Bill.

*Phweet!* "Out of bounds!" called the referee. There were 25 seconds left in the match.

Jackie fell to the mat, laying on his side and breathing deeply. Bill bounced up with renewed vigor and marched to the center. Jackie paused before rising, and then rose slowly, as if he were tired. He was playing a trick, emulating his favorite football player, Jim Brown. Brown was the former running back for the Cleveland Browns, who preserved his strength after being tackled so he could go full tilt at the snap of the ball on the next play. *Be like Jim Brown and go hard at the sound of the whistle,* Jackie thought.

But as Jackie dragged his feet going back to the center, doubts crept in. *I have a one-point lead, so I could probably just play defense and win if the referee doesn't call me for stalling,* Jackie thought. Then he remembered a touchdown from the last game of the season that was called back by a penalty. *Never rely of the refs!*

That aggressive plan returned to the front of Jackie's mind. *He who hesitates is lost!* was Jackie's final thought.

The wrestlers returned to the center of the mat for the restart, with both standing on their feet in the neutral position. "Ready?" asked the referee. *Phweet!*

Like Jim Brown at the snap of the ball, Jackie charged with the whistle, taking off like it was the start of an Olympic 100-meter dash. He caught Bill upright. Double leg takedown!

"Two points, Red! Takedown!" screamed the referee.

Jackie released the hold on Bill's legs after they hit the mat and Bill twisted on his stomach before Jackie could throw in a half nelson. Jackie tapped into his energy reserves, noticing that Bill's seemed empty. Jackie rode out the final period.

*Phweet!* The match was over. The final score was Bill Nettles 3 – Jackie James 6.

With the match over, their sportsmanship returned as they stood up.

"Great match," they both said, shaking hands before the referee could so instruct them.

The public address announcer broadcast the results: "By a score of 6 to 3, the winner in the 175-pound weight class and Metro League Champion is Jackie James of Clintonville High School."

"I'll see you next year on the gridiron!" Bill hollered above the crowd noise.

"Yeah, you'll see me all right…you'll see the number on the back of my jersey as I score another touchdown!" Jackie bantered.

The referee commanded both wrestlers to shake hands, and again they did.

As the referee raised Jackie's arm in victory, Jackie relaxed his muscles and a smile spread across his face.

*Metro League Champion, 175*, he thought.

# Historical Snapshot 2-3:

## The History of The Ohio State University and Buckeye Football

- *In 1862, President Abraham Lincoln signed the Land-Grant College Act, or Morrill Act, which provided grants of land to states to finance the establishment of colleges specializing in "agriculture and the mechanical arts." The Ohio Legislature selected Columbus to be the site of Ohio's Land-Grant College, and The Ohio State University was founded in 1870, located on farmland just three and a half miles north of Broad and High. Surrounding the campus are the neighborhoods of the University District.[17] One mile further north is Arcadia Avenue, the east-west road that marks the informal southern boundary of that part of Columbus that is known as Clintonville.*

- *The Ohio State University first put a football team on the field of play in the spring of 1890. The program gained national attention in 1916 for the first time when Chic Harley, a graduate of Columbus East High School, was recruited to play halfback. Ohio State won the Big Ten Conference the next two years, and Chic Harley was a consensus All-American. The Ohio State Buckeye football games became the go-to event, attracting thousands.[18]*

- *In 1919, Chic Harley returned from his duties as an Army Air Pilot in World War I and led Ohio State to its first victory over Michigan. This success, plus a post-war enthusiasm for physical fitness, provided the momentum for the university to build a large football stadium. Ohio Stadium was completed in 1922 at a cost of $1.3 million, all raised through private donations.[19] The building was the first successful steel-reinforced concrete stadium in the world.[20] From 1951 to 1973, the Buckeyes led the nation in attendance 21 times.[19]*

- *In February 1971, Ohio State football was the dominant sport, and the dominant cultural event in Columbus, Ohio. Coach Woody Hayes was at the peak of his popularity. He had led the Buckeyes to National Championships in 1954, 1957, 1961, 1968, and 1970.*

- *His 1968 team won the Rose Bowl and the National Championship. They were led by their "Super Sophomores" Rex Kern (Quarterback), Ron Macejowski (Quarterback), Jack Tatum (Defensive Cornerback), Leo Hayden (Half-Back), John Brockington (Full-Back), Bruce Jankowski (Receiver), Tim Anderson*

*(Defensive Back), Larry Zelinski (Flanker), Jan White (Tight End), Doug Adams (Linebacker), Jim Stillwagon (Middle Linebacker), Brian Donovan (Center), Dick Kuhn (Left Guard), Mark Debevec (Defensive End), and Mike Sensibaugh (Safety). [21, 22] Quite the recruiting class!*

- *On January 1, 1969, these Super Sophomores led the Buckeyes to a victory over OJ Simpson and the USC Trojans, 27 – 16. On January 1, 1971, those talented sophomores were now talented and experienced seniors and ranked #1. However, on that first day of 1971, the Buckeyes lost in the Rose Bowl to the Stanford University Indians, who were led by the 1970 Heisman Trophy winner, quarterback Jim Plunkett. The Stanford University's team name was changed to "Cardinal" in 1972.[23]*

- *The 1970 Buckeyes would be considered National Champions by the National Football Foundation (NFF) who, at the time, awarded their title before bowl games. However, prospects for the 1971 season were uncertain.*

- *In 1973, John Hicks, the Ohio State Offensive Tackle, won the Outland Trophy, the Lombardi Trophy, and finished in second place for the Heisman Trophy, the highest ever by a player other than a back or receiver.[24]*

# CHAPTER 3

★ ★ ★

## Jackie Brings It Home

.......................................................................................................................

### The James Family Home in Clintonville
#### Columbus, Ohio

.......................................................................................................................

## Jackie James, Son of Joshua and Elizabeth James

JACKIE JAMES RODE up front in the family car with his father, Joshua, as they drove home from the Metro League wrestling tournament. When they arrived home, the rear doors of the car flew open and his younger brother, Sam, who was 15, and his only sister, Rachel, just nine years old, ran between the car and the front door to escape the cold night air. Jackie James and his father, Joshua, were close behind. Elizabeth, Jackie's mother, held the front door open to hasten their entry.

"How'd it go?" she asked, closing the front door and then turning off the TV.

"Great!" Sam announced triumphantly, "Jackie won! Our family's first wrestling champion!"

"Oh!" cried Elizabeth. "Jackie, show me your trophy!"

"Well, it's not really a trophy," said Jackie. "It's a ribbon and metal coin, but it's a win!"

"Well, we're still going to place it in the trophy case. Right, Joshua?"

"It'll be no problem," teased Sam. "It's so small, it'll fit between the football trophies. No need to move them!"

Joshua rolled his eyes and replied, "Okay, wise guy, The real question is are you going to try out for wrestling next year?"

"No way. I'm trying to gain weight for football. I'm not gonna lose weight for anything. I'm going all in for football."

"So, Rachel...how did you like it?" asked Elizabeth.

"It was gross!" said Rachel, wrinkling her nose, "All those sweaty guys were pushing and throwing each other around. There were actual drops of sweat on the wrestling mats, and they were rolling around in it! I'm glad I'm a girl, because girls don't wrestle!"

"That's not true!" her mom quickly responded. "One of my friends at church is a female professional wrestler, Ramona Isbell. And she has friends, Babs Wingo and Ethel Johnston,[25] who also wrestle from Columbus."

"Why would anyone want to do that?" asked Rachel.

"For the money!" replied Elizabeth. "They've wrestled in Chicago, California, and even Japan. They make money...*good money.* They're professional athletes, just like the Cleveland Browns."

"Really, Mom? They travel the world?" asked Rachel, her eyes widening.

"Yes. And they're independent money-wise. On their own. Which is what we want for you. But as long as you're living here, there will be that nine o'clock bedtime!"

Jackie laughed as he thought, *I've heard that before!*

"Jackie, bring your medal and let's go downstairs," said Joshua. "Rachel, will you help us choose where it should be placed?"

The trio descended the stairs to the carpeted basement. Joshua opened the tall trophy case that dominated the long left wall of the basement. A small TV was in the corner. A large straight sofa rested against the long right wall.

"Rachel, where should we put it?" asked Joshua.

"I'd say it would look good—um—here," offered nine-year-old Rachel as she laid out the ribbon and metal medallion on the right side. "It balances and it's a special spot all for itself."

"Nice!" said Joshua.

"This is what I want to do when I grow up," announced Rachel. "Be a decorator. I won't be a female wrestler. I don't like sweating. I don't like getting dirty. And I don't like competition."

"I hear you, Rachel," Joshua answered, "but do you know what these trophies represent? Aaron won these trophies playing football for Otterbein College and being their most valuable player for two years. Those on the left are his high school trophies. These trophies represent victories in competition. Football and good grades got your oldest brother into college."

"But Daddy," whined Rachel, "I just want to be a decorator, and I don't need college or competition for that."

Jackie joined in laughing with his father, who pulled affectionately at the bow in Rachel's hair.

Joshua continued, "You will never be able to escape competition…that's just the way things are in America. When you become a decorator, you'll be competing against other decorators for customers. You'll have to compete and win."

"But you and Mom know many people from school, work, and church. I'll just get your friends to give me their business!"

Joshua shook his head. "Oh, sweetheart, everyone who wants anything done for their home usually gets several bids. So you *will* be competing."

"But, Daddy! You let your friend, Isaiah, fix the upstairs bathroom."

"Yes, but I got two other quotes and made sure he knew about it…just to keep him honest."

"I didn't know that," she said, with a half-hearted shrug of her shoulders.

"But the good news is …you can charge more if you have talent," Jackie said.

"Is home decorating a talent?" asked Rachel.

"Yes, sweetheart, it is," replied Joshua.

Jackie closed the trophy case. "Competition can be fun, Rachel. I'll give you an opportunity to win a dollar. I bet you can't climb the stairs…and count…and remember how many steps there are."

Rachel paused for a second as she examined the stairs. She had climbed them hundreds of times. How hard could this be?

"Okay, Jackie, you've got a bet," Rachel said, shaking hands with Jackie.

Joshua smiled and let them play. Rachel approached the stairs and took her first step.

"One, two, three, four," counted Rachel, climbing the stairs.

"Seven, ten, twenty, two, one, eight, zero, four!" shouted Jackie.

"Stop!" cried Rachel, "I lost my count. Daddy, make him stop!"

"Hey, Pops, stay out of this. This is between Rachel and me. Rachel lost the bet. She owes me a dollar."

"That's not fair," cried Rachel as tears grew in her eyes. "Do I really have to give Jackie a dollar?"

"Yup!" Jackie asserted happily.

"I'm not paying," Rachel whined. "You crossed the line. You didn't play fair. You cheated!"

"Hey, no one said I couldn't play, too! It was a competition...you played, I played... you lost, I won. Pay up!"

Elizabeth opened the doorway to the basement. "What's all this shouting?"

"We had a bet and Jackie distracted me. He cheated! It isn't fair!" complained Rachel.

As Elizabeth descended the staircase, Joshua tried to explain the competition but broke into laughter and struggled to finish. "I think Rachel owes Jackie a dollar," he concluded.

"I don't think so," said Elizabeth, reaching the basement floor. "Here, Rachel, hold my hand. No one said you only got one try!"

Counting together, the mother and daughter ascended the stairs.

"One, two, three, four..."

"Eight, six, ten, a million!" Jackie called out, but his heart wasn't in it.

"...eight, nine, ten...eleven!" shouted Rachel.

"Now, Jackie! Give Rachel a dollar!" asserted Elizabeth.

"Okay, Rachel, here you go," said Jackie. "But I hope you understand that you have just completed a competition and won. Did you enjoy it?"

"I enjoyed winning the dollar!"

"C'mon, now, Rachel," pleaded Jackie. "I saw you holding hands with Mom and counting while you climbed to the top. It looked like you were having fun to me."

Rachel ignored her brother. But, as she wiped away her tears with one hand and held the dollar with the other, a grin broke through when Jackie feigned a poke to her belly.

# Historical Snapshot 3-4:

## The History of Columbus Water

- *In 1900, the City of Columbus was smaller than Ohio's other major cities, Cleveland, and Cincinnati. However, with the influx of government employees and students attending The Ohio State University, Columbus expanded.*

- *In 1900, Senator Mark Hanna of Ohio was the most powerful political boss in America. He was the architect of Ohio Governor William McKinley's successful presidential campaigns of 1896 and 1900. He saw himself as the next President in 1904. When McKinley was assassinated in 1901, Theodore Roosevelt became the youngest person to ever be inaugurated. Senator Mark Hanna told Roosevelt to plan to step aside in 1904 so that he (Hanna) could fulfill his perceived destiny.[26]*

- *Also in 1900, author L. Frank Baum wrote his classic book,* The Wonderful Wizard of Oz. *Many people believe it was a political allegory in which the man behind the curtain pulling the levers of control was Mark Hanna, with McKinley playing the Wizard, blowing smoke.[27]*

- *But Hanna's plans ended in 1904 when he died of typhoid fever as a result of drinking Columbus water. In the aftermath of Hanna's death, the City of Columbus launched a plan to install state-of the-art sanitary engineering ideas that would eliminate typhoid, cholera, and other water-borne illnesses. This "Columbus Experiment" was a great success and served as the model for cities all over the world, saving millions of lives.[28] After World War II, as Central Ohio grew, the city and its suburbs were able to get all the water they needed from the City of Columbus.*

- *Soon afterwards, the Columbus City Council recognized this as leverage to control the growth of the suburbs. Columbus began to annex land between the suburbs, which prevented Columbus from being encircled.*

- *Columbus grew from about 40 square miles in 1950 to over 173 square miles in 1975 as a result of 466 annexations.[29] When Columbus would annex a parcel, the students living inside would often attend their old school until the Columbus Public School System could build new schools for them.*

## Growing City, Growing Schools

- *In 1960, the U.S. Census for Worthington Ohio was 9,239; it grew 66% to 15,326 by 1970.[30] But those numbers are for the city proper; they understate the growth within the school system, which also took in students from the unincorporated areas of Franklin County, the county that has Columbus as its capital.[31]*

- *With the increases in population and land area, the Columbus Public Schools also grew. But unlike most urban areas, the boundaries for the city limits of a suburb of Columbus did not always match the boundaries of its school district.*

- *In the 1960s, the Columbus School Board built new high schools on the north side to handle the increasing student population. In 1971, the student population reached its peak at 110,725.[32] Suburban school districts were concerned about losing their students and their tax base to the Columbus Public School System. Anxiety ran high about the future of students living inside the municipal boundaries of the City of Columbus but attending suburban schools.[33]*

# DAY 2

★ ★ ★ ★ ★ ★

**Friday, February 26, 1971**

# CHAPTER 4

★ ★ ★

## The Last Full Practice

.....................................................................................................

**Worthington Monroe High School**

Columbus, Ohio

.....................................................................................................

## Terry Duke, Head Coach, Worthington Monroe Mavericks Wrestling Team

**T**HIS WOULD BE the last day of practice for the season for some or many of the Mavericks. Each wrestler was approaching this practice in their own way. Kenny Lambert, the senior 185-pounder, didn't even show up.

*Well, at least he promised to be there tomorrow,* thought Coach Terry Duke. He looked at his watch. *A few more minutes until practice starts.*

The next day, the Ohio State High School Interscholastic Federation (OHSIF) would be hosting 16 sectional tournaments all over the state of Ohio. It would be the first step in determining the team championship, and the individual state champion in each weight class. All first-string wrestlers were invited to the sectionals, but they had to win their first two matches to make the districts, the next step in the path to making states.

Coach Duke scrutinized his team. Bobby McCoy was staring off in space again. Carlo was joking it up as usual. Gary was with his fellow flyweights, giving Gino and Lawrence "Lonnie" Williams, the Maverick 98-pounder, instruction as they slowly crisscrossed arms and jumped in place.

Lennie, the heavyweight, practiced his hand fighting moves with Assistant Coach Lloyd Bennett. George "Gorgeous George" Bauchmire, the Maverick 119-pounder, was practicing yesterday's new moves on Marky, as his younger brother, Mike "Mikey" McKelvey, the Maverick 126-pounder waited his turn. Nic, the 167-pound senior, was saying hello to everyone, promising to make districts and see them again next week. Wayne "Flex" Fleckman, the 145-pounder, was walking on his hands to warm up. Bruce "Bulldog" Landers, the 155-pounder, was late because of an emergency student council meeting dealing with the dress code.

Coach Duke smiled slowly. It was his favorite time of the season. Great wins and wild upsets were coming. *Coming our way this year,* he hoped. While each individual Maverick wrestler was striving for their own success, Coach Duke was focused on the team's success, as measured by team points scored at the league, sectional, district, and state tournaments. One team point for a victory, two team points for a win by a pin. Tournament team scores climb when a team is tough up and down the lineup, so Coach Duke worked with all of the Mavericks, not just his favorites. By making the team solid at all weight classes, he built his team. The team points would come, and that would matter at tournament time. And, when a team starts to win tournaments, the coach starts to gain a reputation in the sport. Coach Duke was in his second year as a teacher and wrestling coach and wanted to look good for his boss, the Athletic Director, who had hired him. He needed those team points.

Coach Duke blew his whistle and gathered his team for a talk. He gave a short yet sincere expression of gratitude. He put the team through mild calisthenics and then asked the team to practice their favorite escapes, each practice partner going 50% so they could hone their execution. Half the team practiced their moves with their practice partner while the other half ran in a circle outside the gymnasium, through the halls, and up the steps into the balcony. After fifteen minutes, they switched.

When practice was just over halfway done, Coach Duke looked at his watch. He remembered his high school teammate, Sam Mahaffey, who was always trying something new and pulling off the darnedest moves he'd ever seen. *Hey, if Hambone wants to show us his takedown, now would be the time.* He conferred with his assistant coach, Lloyd Bennett, and received agreement.

*Phweet!* "Okay, everybody! Stop what you're doing and grab your practice partner," announced Coach Duke. Hambone is going to show us his 'go-to' takedown move that—um—well—didn't work last Saturday in your final match, did it? You still want to do this?"

"I can explain that, Coach!" said Gary, coming to the front.

"This I gotta hear," said Lennie, triggering some to laughter.

Gary began, "Here's the truth. Coach is right. This move didn't work for me in my final round match because I was up against a wrestler I'd wrestled twice before. But it worked on him twice before that! The sectional tomorrow is full of teams we've never seen…and they've never seen us. Fresh meat! I call this move the shrug-n-under. It combines the shrug as the setup for the duck-under takedown. The setup is everything!"

"That fancy stuff only works for the lightweights," said Bobby McCoy, the 175-pounder. "In the higher weights, the strength moves are everything."

"Bobby, Bobby, Bobby…always with the negative vibes!" chided Gary, imitating Donald Sutherland's character, Oddball, in the movie *Kelly's Heroes.*

"Bobby, come up here and I'll use you as my partner," Gary said.

"There is no way you could take me down with that move, or any move, Hambone," Bobby insisted, drawing cheers from the wrestlers in the middle and upper weight classes.

"You're right! You have 70 pounds more muscle, so you would crush me in an actual match. But Bobby! That's why this is called *practice*," humored Gary. Cheers now came from the flyweights and the welterweights.

"Bobby, what's your record this year?" Gary asked the big-jawed boy, who was chewing hard and exuding the sweet smell of Dubble Bubble. Coach Duke sighed and held out his hand for the gum that everyone knew was banned from the wrestling room.

Bobby spat out the wad of gum and wiped the back of his hand across his sticky mouth. "Five wins, 13 losses."

"So, if you only use strength moves, then what are you gonna used when you wrestle someone who looks like Arnold Schwarzenegger?"

"C'mon up, Bobby, and play along with Hambone," Coach Duke suggested. "He's a senior, so you won't have to put up with him next year!"

Bobby nodded and pushed off from the wall with the foot he'd been resting there.

*Gotta light some fire in Bobby, somehow,* thought Coach Duke as he wrapped the gum in paper torn from his clipboard and shoved it in his pocket.

"Now, Bobby, don't wrestle me—you'd crush me!" Gary pleaded.

"Let me start by showing you the traditional 'duck-under' takedown move.

"Let's start with the neutral position, each getting a collar tie, and then move into the tie-up position."

"Now, right from the start," Gary continued, "the duck-under has a huge flaw.

"From the tie-up, I need to lift Bobby's right elbow so that I can get my head underneath it."

Gary gritted his teeth and pulled up.

"But I can't do it! I'm not strong enough."

"So, I need to trick Bobby into letting me lift his elbow," Gary explained. "I use the shrug to set that up."

The squad moaned.

"I heard that! Okay, you hate the shrug. But we're only using it as a setup, a feint."

"The way I throw this shrug move is by putting inward pressure on Bobby's right elbow and downward pressure with my collar tie as I push him away and down," said Gary.

Gary stepped backward with his right leg and made a sincere effort to shrug Bobby. Bobby played along, stumbling away like a drunken sailor.

"Now, pair up and practice this shrug." Gary moved amongst the team members and made sure this first step was perfected. The setup was everything.

*He's setting up to be a coach someday!* thought Coach Duke.

"But keep in mind that this shrug can be an effective move at the end of a match when you're ahead by a point or two and need to eat the clock. The referees will never call stalling if you are active, and the shrug is a safe way to be active," said Gary. "Practice this shrug move a few times so it will be a believable ruse."

"Okay," said Gary, "Let's move on to the next part of the move. Here's the key to this shrug-n-under move.

"When your opponent feels your inward pressure on his elbow, he will push back.

"When you feel the outward pressure with your left hand, it will lift easily…

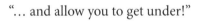
"… and allow you to get under!"

With that, Gary ducked under the arm and stepped forward with his left leg.

Bobby's instinctive reac-
tion was to sprawl away as if
he were defending against a
double leg takedown. As Bobby fell flat on the mat, Gary
moved easily behind him, able
to finish the takedown without
cutting the corner.

"Two points, Hambone!" called Gino, the 112-pounder.

"I let you have it, Hambone," Bobby insisted.

"I know you did," said Gary, only for Bobby. "Thanks, buddy! I owe you one."

Coach Terry Duke stepped forward and announced, "Okay, guys! Start from the
tie-up position and practice this move for five more minutes. Then, we'll wind up practice and Assistant Coach Bennett will have some important information about tomorrow's logistics."

The wrestlers paired off, working on the elbow-pressure setup and the big left step.
Bobby's practice partner, Nic, the 167-pounder, shook off the need for this move and
let Bobby practice all five minutes on offense. Assistant Coach Lloyd Bennett helped
Bobby get it, so Gary moved on to help others.

*Phweet!* "That's it for the shrug-n-under," said Coach Duke, "Thank you, Hambone.
Now, here's some crucial information for tomorrow. You'll get a three-pound allow-
ance, like last week. Lonnie, you wrestle in the 98-pound weight class, so you will need
to weigh in at 101 or less. Have you ever weighed that much in your life, Lonnie?"

The team laughed, happy for Lonnie that he never experienced hunger the day
before weigh-ins. The sophomore weighed only 95 pounds, even after a full meal. Nic,
Bobby, and Mikey, the 126-pounder, were all in a similar position. Nic "wrestled up" at
167 because he didn't want to lose the weight essential for football. Bobby McCoy could

drop the weight to wrestle at 167, but since he couldn't beat Nic, he was stuck at the higher 175-pound weight class, wrestling against stronger opponents. Mikey's situation was similar.

"Weigh-ins will begin at 8:00 a.m. tomorrow," continued Coach Duke. "Be here at 6:45 a.m. so that we can all board the bus together at 7:00 sharp for the ride to Broadleaf High School."

"Coach, what can you tell us about Broadleaf High School and the tournament?" asked Carlo.

"Well, first of all, understand that all conferences, including the Metro League, will be sending wrestlers to this sectional. The good news is that Broadleaf High School is the most diverse of all the Metro League high schools. It will be like going to an Ohio State basketball or football game. Tell your friends and parents to come and cheer for us. And don't think we're something special here at Worthington Monroe High School. Remember, this very building, like Broadleaf, is located within the boundaries of the City of Columbus. One day, our school's name could be *Columbus* Monroe High School."

"How's that possible?" asked Lennie.

"It's called 'annexation,'" replied Coach Duke.

The team stood still, their eyes locked on Coach Duke, who continued, "Look—I have really enjoyed coaching you this season. And I know you've learned more than just wrestling moves. You've shown up here for practice day after day. That's dedication. You're in charge of yourself making weight tomorrow. That's responsibility. And you learned to be a team."

All Maverick eyes were on Coach Duke.

"You have a choice tomorrow. Make the right decision. Choose to get along with all people," said Coach Duke. "And don't say anything about politics. Whatever your opinion is…keep it to yourself."

Coach Duke paused and took a deep breath. Then, he shouted, "Don't stir up any trouble! Am I clear?"

The team nodded in silence.

"Now, let's move on to some lighter matters. Let's see what the fine gentlemen who work on the seeding committee have dealt us. Before I read the seedings, keep in mind that this is the sectional tournament. There are no second chances. There are no wrestlebacks. You need to win your first two matches to make districts."

At each of the 16 sectionals across the state the next day, there would be 16 wrestlers in each of 13 weight classes. The top four in each weight class were seeded. A seeded wrestler would not have to face another seeded wrester until round three, the semi-finals…at which point both would have qualified for districts. A wrestler who lost in round one or round two—their season was over.

Coach Duke smiled and stood on his tiptoes. "But there's good news. If you are unseeded, you have a fifty-fifty chance of drawing another unseeded wrestler in the first round. That's a chance for a team point!" Coach Duke began reading the report from the seeding committee:

"Hambone—#1. You need to win your weight class tomorrow to get the #2 or #3 seed in the districts." Coach Duke was pleased when Gary nodded in confirmation.

Both knew that Alexander Daniels of Bishop Watterson would get the #1 seed at the district tournament in the 105-pound weight class, having beaten Gary earlier in the season. But being a #2 or #3 seed would put Gary in the bottom half of the bracket, safely away from Daniels until the final round. Both district finalists make states. Coach Duke knew this was Gary's goal, along with at least three others.

"Gino—#3. Nice job, Gino! Getting to the league finals helped you.

"George—#3 also. Congratulations! Your strong victory in the league semi-finals gave you a boost. This is the first tournament where you are seeded as high as Gino. Nice work, both of you. You're both in the lower part of the bracket, away from the #1 seed, until the finals.

"Marky—#4. That's lower than I wanted, but you will still get unseeded wrestlers the first two rounds."

"Carlo—#4. That's a drop for you. In fact, you're dropping like a stone. Your reputation is getting around, Carlo. Some of the other coaches were calling you Carlo Rossi, like the winemaker —"

"Now, Coach," interrupted Gino, "if they really knew Carlo, they'd know he likes beer!"

"Wine, too!" yelled Carlo as his teammates failed to suppress their laughter.

"Better not let me catch you with any of that stuff outside your home, Carlo. You'd be off the team in a second. For cryin' out loud, Carlo!" Coach Duke whined. "I wish I had half your talent when I was in high school! With your talent and my work ethic, I could have made states with one arm tied behind my back!"

"And if I was a heavyweight like you were, I could eat and drink all I wanted and never worry about making weight," countered Carlo.

Coach Duke looked skyward and shook his head. "Carlo, I'm trying to reach you, here, but I'm at my wit's end. I'm grasping at straws! Heck, take up cigarettes…it might cut down on your appetite and help you lose weight."

Since that ship had sailed long ago, the team totally lost it. If cigarettes were the answer, Carlo would have been conference champion the previous Saturday.

"Flex—#3," said Coach Duke, getting back to the report.

"Lennie—#2 Seed at Heavyweight. Congratulations, Lennie, you've earned that. By rights, you should easily qualify for districts, and maybe states. You'll be the last match of the first round, and I predict the last match of the tournament also, when you'll be wrestling for the heavyweight championship." Coach Duke stepped back. "And now, some words from Coach Bennett."

"As Coach Duke said, be here tomorrow at 6:45 a.m.," began Assistant Coach Lloyd Bennett. "Everyone must ride the team bus to Broadleaf for the weigh-ins. There is a break, a two or three-hour break, between the third and the final round. The team bus will return here after the third round, sometime between 3:00 p.m. and 4:00 p.m., so that you won't have to stay all day. We'll have a team meeting after the third round and confirm plans for everybody. Remember! Team meeting at the end of the third round. The final round begins at 7:00 p.m."

"Where?" asked Marky.

"Good question. I'll have my wife gather all the families into one group in the stands. Find that group," Coach Duke said.

"What do you want us to do when we're not wrestling, Coach?" asked Bobby.

"There's not enough room in the stands for the wrestlers, so go out into the hallway or roll around on the warm-up mat," Coach Duke replied.  Coach Bennett and I will be inside the gym coaching and scouting your competition. Listen to the announcer for the call of your match number, which is listed on the bracket sheets. For example, if your first-round match is Match 34, then subtract 10 and move to the warm-up area when Match 24 is announced. Any final questions?"

"Hey, Coach!" Gino said, "can you give us a little motivational speech here to fire us up for tomorrow's big tournament?"

"Well," Coach Duke began, "at this point of the season, it's basically one loss and you're done. From now on, it's all about staying alive and moving forward in the sectionals, districts, and states. At this point, it's up to each of you to find your own motivation. Whatever got you motivated in the past, use that. And, besides, I'm not paid any extra if any of you keeping winning and we keep practicing, so here's your chance to get me to work for free. How's that, Gino?  Practice is over."

"Worst motivational speech ever," Gino whispered to Gary as they began picking up their gear.

"I was hoping for George Scott's speech in *Patton*," said Gary.

Sparky, the team's manager, stepped forward. "Guys, it has been my pleasure to serve as your manager. But you know if I was any kind of wrestler, if there was any weakness up or down the line, I'd be in there tomorrow instead of you. When you walk on the mat tomorrow, know that I will be there with you. That's the Maverick spirit. We win together as a team. Each of you can win your first-round match. That's all I want you to think about. All of you are starting a new season. The past is irrelevant. The team needs you. A win gets us a team point and a pin gets us two. I've never seen the Mavericks lead any tournament in team points. Ever. I'm not predicting we will win this sectional tournament, but no one is as solid as us up and down the line. We can take the lead in team points at the end of the first period. That's our goal. It's the next step for Maverick wrestling."

The Mavericks cheered their support for the goal. Then, they circled around Sparky and pounded his back in appreciation. Then, as dictated by last-day-of-practice tradition, the Mavericks carried Sparky to the showers and threw him in. He pretended to be upset.

Coach Duke recalled that Sparky had performed a spontaneous rescue speech last year. Coach Duke had encouraged him to do it again this year, with gusto.

*I love this team's camaraderie. Maybe we'll do well tomorrow! I want this for when I shake hands with the Athletic Director at the end of the school year,* thought Coach Duke.

## Historical Snapshot 4-5:

### Enveloping Events in Sports and Politics

- *On April 15, 1947, Jackie Robinson walked onto Ebbets Field in Brooklyn, New York as the starting first baseman for the Brooklyn Dodgers.[34]*

- *In both the 1952 and 1956 elections, Dwight Eisenhower won in a landslide, garnering 55% and 57% of the popular vote, respectively. Nevertheless, in both elections he lost the southern states of Kentucky, North Carolina, South Carolina, Georgia, Alabama, Mississippi, and Arkansas.[35, 36] If political capital is the power and influence that politicians build up with the public because of successful programs or policies, then President Eisenhower had plenty. He was the military leader of allied forces in World War II, and the president who ended the Korean War in 1953. President Eisenhower had political capital to spend.*

- *Eisenhower was uniquely positioned at a moment in history, and, with zero political risk, he could have brought into effect tremendous progress in the Civil Rights Movement. There was no downside, especially considering that in 1956, he won 40% of the African American vote.[37] If he had championed the nascent Modern Civil Rights Movement, his popularity would have brought along most white Americans. It would have been a uniting moment in American history, a chance to sweep away the old policies of discrimination. A golden opportunity lost.[38] President Eisenhower did intervene to ensure the integration of a high school in Little Rock, Arkansas in 1957. But he did little else.*

- *On October 16, 1968, Tommie Smith and John Carlos protested the slow pace of progress by raising a black-gloved fist, the Black Power Salute, during the playing of the American national anthem after winning gold and bronze medals, respectively, in the 200-meter dash at the Mexico City Olympics. Smith and Carlos were banned from the remainder of those Olympics, but they kept their medals.[39, 40]*

- *The Ohio State University had a long tradition of recruiting and playing African Americans on their football teams. Bill Willis, born in Columbus, played for Ohio State's first National Championship team in 1942. After serving in World War II, he joined his college coach, Paul Brown, on the 1946 Cleveland Browns professional football team. Willis and teammate Marion Motley became the first African Americans to play professional football, playing their first game in September 1946…seven months before Jackie Robinson took the field in Brooklyn.[41, 42]*

- *Woody Hayes became Head Coach at Ohio State in 1951, and recruited African Americans from the start, including Jim Parker, the All-American and future NFL Hall-of-Famer, who played for the Buckeyes on Woody's 1954 National Championship team.*

- *On March 19, 1960, the Ohio State Buckeye's Men's Basketball team won the NCAA Championship at the Cow Palace near San Francisco, with two African Americans in their starting line-up, Senior Joe Roberts and Sophomore Mel Nowell. Their fellow starters were Larry Siegfried, John Havlicek, and Jerry Lucas.*

- *In 1969, Woody Hayes hired Rudy Hubbard as Ohio State's first African American Assistant Coach in football. He was given the responsibility for coaching the running backs. Woody assigned Rudy to recruit in southern Ohio.*

- *But in Ohio in the 1960s, events were not always friendly for African American coaches. One night, after a long day of work, Rudy searched for a motel in a southern Ohio town. At the first place he stopped, he was told there were no vacancies. A passerby advised him to "try the black side of town." Due to this undue harassment, Woody changed his recruiting territory to the Columbus city high schools, the states of Maryland and Virginia, and Washington DC. In 1974, he was appointed as the head coach at Florida A&M. He coached the team to a 11-0 record in 1976, and to a 12-1 record in 1978, capturing the first-ever NCAA Division I-AA Title.[43]*

- *By February 1971, most major colleges had begun offering African American high school athletes full-ride athletic scholarships for playing football or basketball. The University of Alabama had recruited Wilbur Jackson to become a member of their football team in 1970. However, since freshmen were not allowed to play varsity, he was sitting in the stands on that Saturday afternoon in September 1970 when the University of Southern California (USC) brought its integrated team to play Alabama in Birmingham. Freshmen were not allowed to play varsity football until the fall of 1972.[44]*

- *Author Steven Travers wrote about that USC – Alabama game in his book,* One Night, Two Teams: Alabama vs. USC and the Game That Changed a Nation. *He wrote:*

  > *"In the sweltering heat of September of 1970, the USC Trojans and the University of Alabama's Crimson Tide played a game that defined the emancipation of the South from its sordid history of racial segregation. When USC's black running back Sam "The Bam" Cunningham ran roughshod all over the all-white Crimson Tide, more than a football game was won." [45]*

- *USC won by the score of 42 – 21 while gaining an astounding 559 yards on offense. At that time, George Wallace (who said "Segregation today, segregation tomorrow, and segregation forever" in 1963) was still the Governor of Alabama. But the common man in Alabama who had voted for Wallace wanted football victories more than segregation. Alabama coach "Bear" Bryant wanted to recruit African Americans openly and unapologetically. Since Bryant was more popular than Wallace, the lopsided loss prevented Wallace from intervening.*

- *In February of 1971, opportunities for African Americans were opening up, with the entertainment and sporting industries leading the way. Things were moving far more slowly than the African American community wanted or deserved, given that it was 23 years after Jackie Robinson's debut. But, sadly, the rate of change was still too fast for some white Americans, and thus, unfortunately, there was still some resistance.*

# CHAPTER 5

★ ★ ★

## Jackie Meets Woody

..............................................................................................................

**Columbus Clintonville High School**

Columbus, Ohio

..............................................................................................................

## Joshua James, Father of Jackie James

THE COLUMBUS CLINTONVILLE High School, a grand brick building with concrete highlights, was completed in 1921. Along with its football field, the school was built on the north side of Acadia. The east-west road is still, to this day, the informal southern boundary of Clintonville.

Joshua James moved his family to Clintonville in the summer before Jackie's freshman year. His son's athletic success and engaging personality allowed him to make friends easily. His wife Elizabeth developed an informal communication network with the other wrestling team mothers, and they were fortunate to have Lydia Flower, the principal's secretary, as their ringleader.

On this particular afternoon, Joshua James arrived home from his shift at Buckeyes Steel Castings and was surprised when his wife shooed him out the door again, sending him to the Clintonville High School front office. Usually when this happened, it was because his paycheck for his part-time weekend work at the school was ready for pick-up. But today was different. It was the moment that Joshua had hoped would arrive. Ever since Jackie's football team had won the Metro League title and Jackie made All-District halfback, interest in his son had developed and grown among college coaches. But this was special. Woody Hayes was coming!

"He's here!" announced Lydia to the office staff, looking out the window and seeing Woody Hayes, the Ohio State Head Football Coach, and his assistant coach, Rudy Hubbard, ascending the front stairwell. Turning her head to the principal, she said, "Your two o'clock appointment is here!"

When the Buckeye coaches entered the front office, the principal greeted them and introduced the office staff, and also Ed Lawson, the Clintonville football and wrestling coach. The principal then invited the visitors and his coach into his inner office, where he delivered the good news about Jackie's high school records and coursework. Coach Lawson told the coaches about Jackie's heart, his will to win.

A few minutes later, Joshua entered the Front Office and smiled when he saw Lydia waving him over. She opened the principal's office door and introduced Joshua James to the group. As the coaches stood and shook hands with Joshua, the principal locked eyes with Lydia and smiled, pleased that their plan had worked so well.

"I heard you might be here for my son, Jackie. Is that right?" asked Joshua James.

"Yes, indeed we are," said Woody, "and I must congratulate you for the job you've done getting Jackie prepared for college. Your son's education and the completion of his college degree will be very important to us."

*Important words,* thought Joshua, nodding in agreement. *Now let's talk football.*

"Education will be very important to Elizabeth and me," Joshua agreed. "But I'd also like to ask you a question about some football matters. Would that be okay?"

"Of course," replied Woody, "What's on your mind?"

"My oldest son played football at Otterbein College," Joshua said. "Sometimes he played halfback and sometimes fullback. But Jackie's too small to play fullback…and Ohio State is known for its fullbacks."

"Well, this past year, we used both running backs, John Brockington at fullback and Leo Hayden at halfback, and both had great years," said Woody. "We put our players where they will have success…be able to execute. We won't be asking Jackie to play fullback, but he will have to block on plays when he is not carrying the ball. But whatever position on the field he plays, if he comes to Ohio State, that field of play will be here in Columbus, at the Horseshoe."

Joshua nodded slowly and allowed a slight smile.

"So, who's Jackie's favorite professional football player?" asked Coach Hayes.

"Without a doubt, it was Jim Brown, until he retired to make the *Dirty Dozen* movie."

"Well, we won't promise Jackie a movie career," laughed Woody, "but a career after football is always an important consideration. Columbus is a great city. There are many Ohio State athletes that have great lives in Columbus when their playing days are over."

Joshua turned towards Rudy and began, "In the end, it will be Jackie's decision… and I'll back that choice." When Joshua finished, he was looking Woody in the eyes.

As if that were meant to be the final word, the last bell of the day rang out and the hallways filled with noise.

"Would it be possible to talk with Jackie today?" asked Woody, standing up.

"As a matter of fact, Jackie is heading to wrestling practice right now," said Coach Lawson. "Let's join him…which I must do anyways because I'm also his wrestling coach. I'll give you a tour and then we'll go to the wrestling room. Joshua, please join us!"

When Joshua and the three coaches entered the wrestling room, the Clintonville team was on the mat, stretching. Coach Lawson raised the whistle to his lips and blew it softly; the team had noticed the special visitors and already gone silent. "I have a special treat for you today. I'd like to introduce Coach Woody Hayes and Coach Rudy Hubbard of the Ohio State Buckeyes. Can anyone tell me which sport they coach?"

All eyes turned to Jackie as laughter broke out, finding humor in the obvious. Even Woody and Rudy enjoyed a chuckle, breaking the ice and the awe.

The wrestlers were also familiar with Joshua, as he worked at their school whenever there was a Saturday home dual wrestling match. Joshua stood inconspicuously to the side.

"I've asked Coach Hayes to share his thoughts with us as we prepare for the sectional tournament tomorrow at Broadleaf. Coach Hayes, would you like to share a few words?"

"Thank you, Coach Stuart. People always ask me what kind of players I'm looking for. Well, the most important thing is that they must have a winning attitude. Winning is the epitome of team effort. I'm looking for players who are team-oriented…and players who have self-esteem. Sometimes people ask me if those standards are found in all homes. I tell them that I find good homes wherever I go. The amount of money in the home has very little to do with it. A good home has two things: the kid knows that he is wanted, and there is discipline in that home. He believes in the people who take care of him. But if a player comes from a bad home or no home at all, well, he didn't get to choose that. I'll take him and give him a double chance if he appears to rise above those circumstances." [46]

"And I will help him rise," Coach Hayes promised. "All my freshman players meet with me on Sunday mornings to learn 'Word Power.' And one of the words we learn is 'apathy.' I don't want you on the football field if you show any signs of apathy. Apathy…avoid it like the plague. It's the damnedest thing in the world. And you'll run into those people who will say 'Why play football?'…'Why wrestle?'…'You work too hard.'…'C'mon and have a joint with me.' And he'll sit there and look at his shoe for an hour." [46] Joshua noticed that there were some giggles and guffaws from the team, but not from his son, who stayed focused on Coach Hayes' words. Joshua wondered if those who'd laughed the loudest were perhaps overly familiar with the apathetic crowd, possibly even a member of that group.

"And he's thinking great thoughts," Coach Hayes satirized. "I'm not kidding you. And those kids are apathetic as hell, and they're going nowhere. And they take a lot of people with them. If you only learn this one word today, *apathy*, learn to avoid it like the plague. And you'll see students who are apathetic all over the school. These people have never done one thing for civilization." [46]

The wrestlers returned warm applause, proud to have the coach in their wrestling room and talking straight to them.

"Thank you, Coach Hayes," concluded Coach Lawson, with a note that suggested it was time to get to work. "Let's start warming up."

When Coach Hayes quietly asked Coach Lawson a question, he responded, "By all means. Jackie, c'mon up here."

The Buckeye coaches led Jackie and Joshua to the hallway. Joshua shook hands again with the coaches and left his son to talk, alone.

## Jackie James, Columbus Clintonville 175-Pounder

"Jackie, Coach Hubbard and I would like to congratulate you for being named to the All-District team," said Coach Hayes. "You've had a great year, and we look for great things next year also."

"Th-thanks…Coach Hayes," Jackie stammered, "… and Coach Hubbard."

"I was sincere in what I was saying about wanting team-oriented players. I won't promise you playing time. But if you come to Ohio State, I can promise that you will get a fair shake, a chance to show your talents. I also want you to consider that we recruit excellent offensive linemen. So, if you carry the ball for the Buckeyes, you'll have a fine offensive line blocking for you."

"We know you have options, Jackie," Coach Hayes continued, "but ask yourself what teams have had the All-American offensive linemen like we have had at Ohio State. You remember our offensive tackles, Dave Foley and Rufus Mayes, both All-Americans on the 1968 National Championship team, don't you? Our next All-American offensive tackle will be John Hicks, who won the starting job this past year as a sophomore. We have an excellent tradition at Ohio State with our running backs winning the Heisman Trophy, but they did not do it on their own. In football, you win with people, and we have the people on the offensive line that you will want to play with."

The message resonated. Jackie knew all about John Hicks, the black offensive tackle from Cleveland.

"Thank you, Coach Hayes," replied Jackie. "I promise I will think about what you have said."

Hayes clapped Jackie's shoulder. "Okay, son, we'll leave you now so you can join your teammates. Oh! …and good luck in the tournament tomorrow!"

"I'll be there to watch," said Coach Hubbard, "and I'll be bringing the offensive coordinator."

A grin spread across Jackie's face as he shook hands with the coaches. He was on Ohio State's radar! The grin stayed in place the entire practice.

In the locker room after practice, as Jackie was getting back into his street clothes, Joe Clarke, his friend, practice partner, and fellow black wrestler on the team, sat down next to him.

"Jackie, do you remember that guy who came to school and told us about the local plumbers union opening up its apprenticeship program?"

"Last fall? No, wait. It was the year before that. Sophomore year, right? I remember because my pop's friend is a member of that union and I've heard them talk shop."

"Do you remember the guy who spoke? I think he was someone who hires the plumbers. He said that anyone who passed their test to be an apprentice would automatically get admitted into that apprenticeship program."

"Yes, I remember. We were excited! I mean...pass the test and you're in? It was never that easy in the past."

"Well," explained Joe, "my older brother took that test and passed it, but they still refused to let him in!"

"What? Did they tell your brother why?"

"They said his test results weren't high enough, even though he passed. They told him others scored higher, so the others were let in. But that wasn't what the guy said at the assembly."

"Yeah, you're right," Jackie agreed. "Is there any way to fight it?"

"My brother filed a lawsuit with the EEOC...well, not him alone...but with the local NAACP. They filed it against the plumbers union to force them to open up the apprenticeship program to everyone."

"Did he win?"

"Don't know. Still tied up in court!"

"That was more than a year ago!"

"I know!" said Joe. "A bunch of us are planning to hold a rally on Monday after school, at the flagpole. A professor at Ohio State, Charles Ross, says he's coming to join us. I was wondering if you would also join us."

"I don't know...I might still have wrestling practice next week, depending on to-morrow," Jackie said, his voice trailing off.

"It's not fair," Joe said, his voice rising. "If they say you can have a slot if you pass a test, and then you pass the test, then you should have that slot. Period."

"But Joe," Jackie said, analyzing the situation, "what if there are more people who pass the test than there are slots available?"

"I don't know," Joe responded, "but that's not how they explained it."

"My pop's friend, Isaiah, told us that some contractors are starting to use nonunion construction workers, so getting jobs at the hiring hall is more difficult, especially for those with lower seniority…and especially now with the brewery completed. I don't see them bringing in a flood of new apprentices."

"I'll have to think about this," continued Jackie. "It's good news that all are allowed to take the test. That's better than it used to be. A chance to compete—"

"Jackie…'the times they are a-changin,'" interrupted Joe. "We need to stand up and demand fair treatment."

"I hear you, Joe, but my family chooses to follow Dr. King. He pushed for change peacefully."

"Dr. King is dead…and so are his ideals. Today, it's all about Black Power and protest."

Jackie stared at the slogan on Joe's T-Shirt, *Free Angela*. Jackie thought, *What's the right thing to do?*

"You remember what happened to Tommy Smith and John Carlos at the last Olympics?" asked Jackie. "They were booted off the Olympic team…forever…and sent home early."

"I hear you, Jackie, but you were the one who mentioned 'choosing.' It's time to choose."

"And I hear you, Joe. I'll tell you Monday."

# Historical Snapshot 5-6:

## Enveloping Events in Columbus

- *The local plumber's union in Columbus, Ohio is known officially as Local 189 of the United Association of Journeymen and Apprentices of the Plumbing and Pipefitting Industry of the United States and Canada. In 1968, members of this union conceived a plan to write a book about the history of the union, and they selected Richard Schneirov to be its author. Here are two excerpts from that book describing events from the 1960s:*

   > *"Before the Civil Rights Act of 1964 took effect in the construction industry, Local 189 … was a loosely knit clique limited to relatives of those already in the union. This 'club atmosphere' furthered the transmission of skills and customs from generation to generation, but it excluded all outsiders, men and women, black and white, who were potentially qualified and might want to work at the trade.*

   > *Meanwhile, the union's apprenticeship program had begun to feel the full effects of affirmative action. In 1969, a representative from the Limbach Company, while touting the apprenticeship program at Columbus high schools, mistakenly announced that anyone passing an aptitude test would be hired automatically. He failed to mention that applicants would be placed on a list ranked by test scores. When a black teenager passed the test and was not accepted into the program because he was low on the list, he filed a lawsuit with the EEOC (Equal Employment Opportunity Commission)."*

   > *"In July 1972, after spending $15,000 in court fees, the JAC (Joint Apprenticeship Committee of Local 189) lost the case. The JAC accepted a ten-year consent decree from U.S. District Court Judge Karl B. Rubin, which required the JAC to take in black applicants as its first ten apprentices and accept 11 to 12 percent black applicants in future entering classes."[47]*

- *Black History Month was first proposed by black educators and the Black United Students at Kent State University in February of 1969 The first celebration of Black History Month took place at Kent State one year later, in February of 1970.[48]*

- *In February of 1971, the Columbus Public Schools first celebrated Black History Month. Sadly, the program intended to promote black pride encountered resistance. The* Columbus Evening Dispatch, *the local afternoon newspaper, reported the following stories:*

  > *"Principals in at least three Columbus high schools are scheduled to meet on Monday with student leaders to ensure that there will be no recurrence of recent student flare-ups. All told, eight students have been suspended."*[49]

  > *"At Linden-McKinley, several fights broke out during a Black History Week assembly when four white students were alleged to have thrown anti-black literature from the balcony during the assembly."* [49]

  > *"At West High School, an assault on a student has led to the suspension of four students and the cancellation of the West – Eastmoor basketball game."*[49]

  > *"At Central High School, about 75 students refused to return to classes in protest over the lack of a special program for Black History Week. Central principal Calvin Park will meet with black student leaders next week to discuss their complaints."*[49]

- *In February of 1971, Angela Davis, at the time a member of the Communist Party USA, was in jail and on trial for three capital felonies, including conspiracy to commit murder. In 1970, guns belonging to her were used in an armed takeover of a courtroom in Marin County, California. Four people were killed. She was held in jail for over a year. In 1972, an all-white jury returned a verdict of not guilty. The fact that she owned the guns used in the crime was judged insufficient to establish her culpability, her blameworthiness.*[50]

- *On April 26, 1968, in the wake of the assassination of Dr. Martin Luther King, Jr., members of the Black Student Union at Ohio State University occupied the Administration Building, located at that time in Bricker Hall. They entered the building peacefully for a scheduled meeting with OSU administration officials to discuss issues important to the Black Student Union.*

- *The issue of the day was the racial discrimination against black students applying for off-campus housing in the University District. When the members of the Black Student Union refused to leave after the meeting, and occupied the building for 10 hours, it was deemed to be a takeover, and not a peaceful protest. Thirty-four African American students were indicted. Most of the charges were dropped, but six of the thirty-four were expelled. There was no property damage.* [51, 52, 53]

- *On January 30, 1971, the Columbus City Council, by a unanimous vote, passed into law a landmark ordinance, sponsored by Dr. John Rosemond, which would penalize those found guilty of practicing discrimination in housing, employment, and public accommodations in the City of Columbus.* [54]

★ ★ ★ ★ ★ ★

**Saturday, February 27, 1971**

# CHAPTER 6

★ ★ ★

## The Fathers' Advice

The Morning of Tournament Day,
on the Way to Meet the Team Bus

## Robert "Bobby" McCoy, Son of Rick and Georgia McCoy

**B**OBBY WOKE TO the clanging of the frying pan against the kitchen sink. He rolled out of bed, threw on his street clothes from the day before, and packed his gym bag. He considered taking his Joe Weider bodybuilding magazine but threw it on the table by his bed. He headed down the hallway past the empty bedroom of his older brother Dick. Soon, he was downstairs where his parents, Rick and Georgia McCoy, were eating breakfast. His mother was admiring her new kitchen appliances.

"Morning, Mom. Morning, Dad." A quizzical look passed over Bobby's face as he entered the kitchen and observed his mother's reverie. He couldn't for the life of him understand her fascination with what he thought were ugly pieces of kitchen equipment. "Hey, Mom, tell me again—what's the name of that color?" asked Bobby.

"They're avocado," said his mother with a satisfied smile. "It's very popular."

"With whom?" asked Bobby and his father in unison. Bobby's mother dismissed them with a wave of her hand.

When Bobby stopped laughing, he said, "But really, Mom, thanks for not calling me down for breakfast. I didn't want to be tempted by food today. I have to make weight this morning."

"I thought so. But don't worry about that, Bobby. You never have problems making weight!" said his mother.

"Yeah, but it's tournament day and I don't want to let the team down. I might draw an unseeded wrestler like myself and have a chance to score a team point. I want to be ready."

"All right, let's go!" said Rick, grabbing a last piece of bacon as he stood up to leave.

They walked down the front steps to their car, parked on the street. This one was for running errands. The new family car was in the garage.

Generally, on tournament days, Bobby's father was full of wisdom and advice for his son. They usually turned the music up during the ride and talked off any nervousness Bobby felt. But today, Rick was silent, seemingly stewing. Out of nowhere, he let out a sigh.

"The president of the union gave me an update on that stupid lawsuit this morning—the one that was filed against our apprentice program." Bobby had heard a lot about this lawsuit, including the story about the union contractor who'd visited all the Columbus high schools, incorrectly informing the students that just passing a special test designed by an Ohio State professor would allow entry into the apprentice program.

"It's been in the rules forever. We take only a certain number...those with the highest scores, not everybody who passes! Plus, well, well...I mean, we like to help those applicants who appreciate what it means to get to be a member of our union, if you catch my drift. We know a lot about the test. We're not cheating...just helping our own."

Rick was getting onto his soapbox, a speech his son had heard many times. "We do have black plumbers in our union, and they're good plumbers because they have previous experience. But we can't let just anybody who passes the test become an apprentice."

"Why not?" asked Bobby.

"There would be too many! And, with the Anheuser-Busch brewery completed, we don't even have work for all our current members. Guys like me with seniority are busy, but not the young guys. I wish we had new construction work, but that has all gone to scab plumbers, just like the new home electrical work went to scab electricians like your uncle."

"Hey! Uncle Ron's okay! He doesn't badmouth you. And without him, I wouldn't have had a job last summer," said Bobby.

"Yeah—well—I'm disappointed that I couldn't get you a plumbing job last summer. I didn't have enough pull. So, you had no other choice but Ron. But I'm working it for this coming summer and then getting you into the apprentice program when you graduate. Your wrestling helps. It'll make you tough, like our business manager, Curt Stettner. A really tough guy. A man's man."

"Did he wrestle in high school?"

"No, but during World War II, when Bastogne was surrounded by Germans, Curt parachuted directly into the fight. That's the kind of tough guy Curt Stettner is. And Curt likes tough guys because the work is hard, and the negotiations with the contractors are even harder."

"Yeah, but Curt sure handled them in '67 during the last strike," said Bobby, knowing it would trigger his dad to retell the story. Bobby knew this would put his father in a good mood.

"You ain't whistling Dixie!" exclaimed Bobby's father. "Curt called the strike when the brewery work was going strong...and then made sure everybody working at the brewery kept working! There was a shortage of plumbers, so the contractors caved. They had to!

"Curt Stettner may be the best union business manager in America. Our membership has doubled, and we now cover all Central Ohio! We've gone from $4.67 an hour before the strike to $8.80 this year. And, we have a 15 cents per hour pension fund! Paid for by the contractors!"

Rick was on a roll, so Bobby just watched, pleased to see his father happy and off his back. "Can you believe that our local members make more than our pipefitting brothers working in New York or San Francisco? And, with double pay for overtime, we make double what the average American makes. Plus, there are future increases already in place, so we're not falling behind this creeping inflation."

Suddenly, Rick went serious. "I want this all for you. That's why I'm pushing for you to get into the apprentice program. I don't want anyone from a Columbus city school taking that away from you."

"Well, I appreciate the new car waiting in the garage!" said Bobby. "If I win my first match today, can I use it to take out Cassie tonight?"

"Nice try, son," replied Rick. "But no."

Rick turned on the radio and the WTVN 610 AM news came on.

> "…more bad news as the South Vietnamese Army has suffered a significant setback in their invasion of Laos. Yesterday, the North Vietnamese overran a South Vietnamese paratrooper base, inflicting severe casualties in what has perhaps been the heaviest fighting of the Indochina War. The effort of the ARVN, the South Vietnamese Army, to cut off the flow of supplies coming down the Ho Chi Minh Trail appears to be in serious jeopardy. Only a week ago, the Nixon administration was claiming the Laotian invasion was painted in success."

Rick reached over to turn the radio off, but hesitated.

> "In Saigon, U.S. Command reported a sharp increase in overall American battle deaths last week. It said that 59 Americans were killed in combat, and another 42 were reported to have died from non-hostile causes."

"Non-hostile causes?! What is that?" screamed Rick, "If you're dead, that sounds hostile to me!"

Bobby nodded. His father had a point.

"Damn those Commies!" snapped Rick. "Commies nearly killed me in Korea and now we're fighting 'em again in Vietnam. If the South Vietnamese army can't beat the Viet Cong, then send the Marines back in! Nixon has been removing our troops from Vietnam and replacing them with South Vietnamese troops…stupid Vietnamization policy! I knew it wouldn't work! No one fights like the U.S. Marines!"

He looked across at Bobby. "Bobby, I don't want you to go to Vietnam…but if you are called, I know you will do your duty…as I did in Korea and as Dick did in 'Nam. Those anti-war hippies are undermining our war effort! We're in the middle of a war, and we're divided? The enemy knows it! What happened at Kent State last year…well, those students deserved it. I can't stand the thought that Dick died for no reason. We *have* to win this war."

Rick glanced at Bobby, trying to make eye contact, but Bobby looked away, gritting his teeth. *The students at Kent State did not deserve it,* Bobby thought. That was the universal feeling at his high school. And the majority of Ohioans agreed. Republican Governor James Rhodes had lost his race for the U.S. Senate in November of 1970. Then Bobby thought of Dick. His mind went numb.

Rick continued his rant. "We preserved democracy for South Korea, and we'll do the same for South Vietnam!"

Bobby didn't see it happening, but let it be.

"But I'm glad I get a chance to see you wrestle today, son. It'll make you a better worker this summer. Toughen you up. I don't want you losing your slot in that program. Remember what I told you…'Winning isn't everything' …"

"It's 'The Only Thing!'" said Bobby, bubbly enough to keep his father happy.

## Jackie James, Son of Joshua and Elizabeth James

Jackie James woke up as the first light of morning brightened the window shade. He stretched his arms and yawned, contorting his entire face. Then, he sat upright to ward off any new rush of sleepiness. A glance at his alarm clock warned him it would be ringing soon, so he turned it off and allowed his younger brother, Sam, to sleep in.

He grabbed his blue jeans and selected the red Otterbein sweatshirt over the purple one. *If the Ohio State coaches do show up, I need to be wearing something red.* He double-checked the contents of his gym bag and zipped it shut. His uniform was ready and so was he. He crept downstairs to the kitchen to find his parents enjoying a private Saturday morning breakfast.

"Want anything?" asked his mother, Elizabeth.

"No, thanks. I've gotta make weight. And I need to hustle over to the school…like now."

"I can take you in a few minutes," said his father, Joshua. "I'll be working there today until about two myself."

"Pops, if it's okay, can we leave now? I mean, I really don't want to watch you guys eat breakfast when I'm starving."

"Okay, Jackie," said Joshua, forking another bite of pancakes into his mouth and leaving a sticky kiss on Elizabeth's cheek as he got up from the table. "Let's go."

Father and son arrived early at the high school parking lot. The radio was tuned to WVKO 1580 AM, and the energizing beat of "Mama's Pearl" [55] swept away Jackie's low-blood-sugar blues.

As the song faded out, Russel Brown, the disc jockey, came on:

> *"That was the Jackson 5 featuring Michael Jackson on WVKO AM 1580, The Rhythm of the City…and can you believe that Michael Jackson is only 12 years old! The Jackson 5 were in Columbus just last month, and WVKO was there to*

*report on it for you, including yours truly. Is Michael a better singer or dancer? I*
*can't make up my mind. But now, it's time for today's news. Take it, Jamie!"*

Jamie's authoritative voice took over the broadcast:

*"At Linden-McKinley High School yesterday, Ohio State professor Charles O.*
*Ross, the Director of the Black Studies Division, was arrested as a result of his and*
*several students' efforts to raise the Black Nationalist Flag at the school. Ross and*
*several students, a teacher and a custodian, were all arrested."* [54]

*"Ten citizens of Columbus were presented outstanding achievement awards*
*as the Association for Negro Life and History climaxed its observance of Black*
*History Week at Columbus East High School. The honorees included Mayme*
*Moore, David White, Grace Steward, Russell Pace, Ernest Mackey, Barbee*
*Durham, Edna Bryce, William Bell, Nimrod Allen, and William Savoy. Congrat-*
*ulations to you all!"* [54]

*"In the sporting pages, Baltimore Orioles outfielder Frank Robinson has been*
*given a $5,000 pay raise to a salary of $130,000 for the 1971 season. Frank led*
*the Orioles to the 1970 World Series crown over the Cincinnati Reds. I still love*
*the Reds…but way to go, Frank!*

*"This is Jamie Franklin for WVKO News, and now back to the music."*

Joshua turned off the radio, thankful for the opportunity to talk with his son, alone.
The school bus hadn't arrived, so they had a few minutes. Jackie unlocked his seat belt
and turned to his father, who cleared his throat.

"I'll be here at the school, working until the mid-afternoon," said Joshua. "I won't
be able to see you wrestle during the day, but I'll be there tonight for the finals, just like
last Saturday."

Jackie smiled. "I understand, Dad. Coach told me yesterday that I'm the #1 seed
and that I need to win the first two matches to make districts. I'm staying focused on
those first two matches. But I also hope you get a chance to see me wrestle tonight."

Jackie continued, "Do you think those Ohio State coaches will show up today?"

"Did they say anything?" asked Joshua.

"Yeah. Coach Hubbard said he would come and bring the offensive coordinator. Do you think they'll actually come?"

"Well—let's see! Let's see if he is a man of his word. I wish I could be there this morning to talk to him."

Jackie raised an eyebrow. "Let's not chase 'em, Pops. Remember that Northwestern contacted me first. And I like Coach Agase. But playing here in Columbus…well… you'd better take *those* Saturdays off!"

Joshua drew in a deep breath and looked Jackie in the eyes. "I'll be there. That's *my word.*"

Joshua put both hands on the steering wheel and looked through the windshield as if looking down the road to Jackie's future. "Watching you play reminds me of watching Jackie Robinson…you both just *loved* to play and it showed. I'm glad I named you after him."

"Pops, tell me what you mean. Did you ever see Jackie Robinson?" asked Jackie.

"Well, here's a story about the first time I ever saw Jackie Robinson play. It was on TV. October 1, 1952. Game 1 of the 1952 World Series…an afternoon game, televised coast-to-coast by NBC.[56]

"In the bottom of the second inning, Jackie Robinson homered to left field…right down the line, and Brooklyn took the lead, 1-0," said Joshua.

"You saw Jackie Robinson hit a home run, live on TV?" asked Jackie.

"Yessir…but that's not the play that sticks in my mind. In the bottom of the sixth inning, Jackie came to bat with Brooklyn holding a 3 – 1 lead. Jackie hit a grounder to the third baseman. Should have been an easy out, but Jackie was *never* an easy out. His speed running to first base forced the Yankee infielder to rush his throw…and it was wild."

"Safe…on an error?" asked Jackie.

"Yessir! Then, once on base, Jackie would take these huge leads off of first base and just dare the pitcher to try to pick him off. When the Yankee pitcher threw to first base to pick-off Jackie, we were surprised when he did!"

"What? Jackie was out?"

"Yes, and then…*no!* At first, Jackie was picked off…but the ball rolled out of the Yankee first baseman's glove during the tag. So, Jackie was safe!"

"Safe?"

"Safe!" thundered Joshua, sticking his arms out as straight as he could inside the car. "And then…as the ball rolled and rolled away, Jackie scampered down to second base. Jackie just destroyed the Yankees' confidence. Catcher Yogi Berra had to call a time out and visit the mound to settle his team down. Those Yankees didn't know if they were a'comin' or a'goin'!"

Joshua tried to catch his breath between his guffaws. "Jackie loved to be on the field… the love of fair play in sports. It's about the only place he could find fair play in 1952."

"Anyways, the final score was Dodgers 4, Yankees 2. And Dodger pitcher Joe Black, who is also black, threw a complete game and got the victory!"

Jackie gazed into space and envisioned the action. There was silence for a moment.

"Pops, remember the news story about that Ohio State Professor Ross getting arrested? Well, my teammate Joe said that Ross will be coming to Clintonville High on Monday for a rally after school and Joe wants me to join in. But Joe didn't mention anything about Ross and his fellow protesters getting arrested. I wonder if he knew. No way I'll be there now."

"Good decision. I think you know, Jackie, that you have a chance for a full-ride athletic scholarship. A wrong choice could cost you that chance. That's just the way it is, for now. But this won't be your last opportunity to take a stand. And, son, there are ways to take a stand without it costing you."

"What do you mean?" asked Jackie.

"Well, here's another Jackie Robinson story you might like. He was required, by his contract with the Dodgers, to avoid any trouble. I mean, he was literally required to keep his mouth shut...in America! But, before he was a Dodger, he made his presence felt."

Joshua adjusted himself in the driver's seat to face his son again. "When Jackie played in the Negro Leagues for the Kansas City Monarchs," he continued, "the team bus routinely traveled throughout the South. One day, running on empty and needing to refill the two large auxiliary tanks on each side of the bus, they pulled into the next gas station. As everyone got out to stretch, Jackie headed for the restroom. The station owner yelled at Jackie and told him the restrooms were for whites only." [57]

"What did he do?" asked Jackie.

"He didn't cause a ruckus. He did an about-face and calmly walked back to the gas pump and shut it off. Then he removed the nozzle from the bus's auxiliary tank and hung it properly on the side of the gas pump. He then declared to the owner that if they couldn't use the restroom, then they would pay for this small amount of gas and move on down the road."

"What did Jackie's teammates say?" asked Jackie.

"Nothing. They just stood there and watched the owner make the next move. The owner, eyeing the large auxiliary tanks, relented. The Monarchs got to use the restroom; the owner got the sale. And I'm guessing that the station owner never told a soul. Jackie got it done...without any problems. Everybody got what they wanted."

The Clintonville school bus turned into the parking lot and approached the waiting cars.

"Here's my ride!" Jackie said. "Bye, Pops!"

"Bye, son. Go get 'em."

Jackie boarded the team bus for the ride to Broadleaf High School. He found his favorite seat and faced forward, thinking of how Jackie Robinson must have felt on the team bus afterwards.

## Historical Snapshot 6-7:

.......................................................................................

### Enveloping Events in Vietnam

- *In February of 1971, the War in Vietnam was still raging. Casualties per year had fallen from a peak of 16,592 in 1968 to…11,616 in 1969…6,081 in 1970…2,357 in 1971…641 in 1972…and 168 in 1973.[58] The reduction in casualties was due to "Vietnamization," a program started in January of 1969, shortly after President Nixon was inaugurated.[59] Its goal was to replace American soldiers with members of the Army of the Republic of Vietnam (ARVN) on the front lines. Until February of 1971, the administration claimed that the program was successful, and that ARVN troops were winning the war. On February 8, 1971, the ARVN began an offensive campaign into the neighboring nation of Laos. The goal of the campaign, known as Lam Son 719, was to disrupt the flow of arms down the Ho Chi Minh Trail, the logistical system that supported the North Vietnamese army, and their ally, the Viet Cong.[60] The early news reports from the field were of ARVN victories. However, on Friday, February 26, 1971, the headline of The* Columbus Evening Dispatch *read:*

### S. Viet Base In Laos Overrun[61]

- *It was the high-water mark for those in America, the Nixon Administration, and the Pentagon who thought the ARVN could win the war and defend their homeland. It was the "Pickett's Charge" moment of the Vietnam War.*

- *In February 1971, the Nixon Administration was considering its options: (1) re-escalate the war by returning American Marines to the front lines, or (2) find an honorable way out that would not look like defeat.*

- *A month after the disastrous Laos invasion by the ARVN, it became increasingly apparent, with each passing day, that the war was un-winnable. The Nixon Administration put its efforts into pulling out of Vietnam. The Nixon Administration adopted a future strategy of containment, not victory, against Communism.*

- *On September 28, 1971, President Nixon signed a draft bill that eliminated the college deferment. The seniors at the February 1971 sectional wrestling tournament who entered college in August or September of 1971 would be re-classified as I-A, "Available for Military Service." None of the wrestlers in the tournament would ever receive a college deferment.[62]*

- *On January 27, 1973, the Paris Peace Accords were signed, and America removed all of its remaining troops from Vietnam. The nation of South Vietnam stood alone. But the peace accord did not bring peace; the war continued between North and South Vietnam. In January 1974, President Thieu of South Vietnam declared that the peace accord was no longer in effect.[63]*

- *In August 1974, President Nixon resigned. In December 1974, the U.S. Congress passed the Foreign Assistance Amendments, which cut off all military aid to Thieu's South Vietnam government in Saigon. This broke the promise made by President Nixon at the time of the signing of the Paris Peace Accords—the promise to use American Air Power to protect South Vietnam.[64]*

- *By the afternoon of April 30, 1975, the armies of North Vietnam and the Viet Cong controlled the city of Saigon, and the war was over. Saigon was renamed Ho Chi Minh City.[65]*

# CHAPTER 7

★ ★ ★

## Maverick Motivations

························································································

The Morning of Tournament Day, on the Way to the
Worthington Monroe School Bus Heading for the
Sectional Tournament at Broadleaf High School

························································································

### Gary "Hambone" Hamilton, Son of Carl Hamilton

GARY HAMILTON AWOKE to the sound of WCOL 1230 AM on his clock radio. He pulled the covers over his ears as the sound of Donnie Osmond singing "One Bad Apple" filled his bedroom. *Still playing that song?* Gary thought, shaking his head. *There must be millions of teenage girls like my sister swooning over the chance to forgive Donnie Osmond for being a bad boy.*

Gary dressed in his blue jeans and Ohio State sweatshirt. He walked down the hallway, past his sisters' bedrooms, and down the half-flight of stairs that led through the foyer into the kitchen. He opened the refrigerator door and thought about grabbing something. It was a drink of water that Gary wanted the most. *Not today,* he thought, closing the refrigerator.

He returned to the foyer to call for his father, then was relieved to see him coming down the stairs.

"Can I drive, Dad?"

"Sure, son. It's your day and we have the time."

A relaxed smile came across Gary's face and he stood up a little straighter. His father was not late today. *This matters to him…like a tee time.*

Gary enjoyed driving his father's Lincoln Continental and kept the radio on WBNS 1460 AM, his father's favorite, as they headed for the high school parking lot.

"When you gonna get a new car, Dad? This one's more than three years old."

"Not yet! It runs like a scared deer!"

Hearing the radio announcer declare the news was coming on, Carl Hamilton turned the volume up:

> *"Unnamed sources inside the White House are concerned about recent developments in Laos. The White House was counting on the policy of Vietnamization to work so that U.S. forces could continue to be withdrawn. From a peak of 550,000 U.S. soldiers in 1968 to about 200,000 now, Vietnamization appeared to be working. However, with this disastrous invasion of Laos by the ARVN, Vietnamization is failing. The U.S. Selective Service draft boards may need more fresh troops than in previous years. The cutoff draft number was 195 the year before. It looks like it might be going back up for those born in 1953, who are now most likely seniors in high school.*

> *"In a related story, politicians are calling for an end to the college deferment for the draft. There are no plans to make changes for this year's lottery for those born in 1952. But the college deferment for 1953 and beyond is doubtful. In a rare moment of cooperation, both political parties have aligned against the college deferment."*

"Holy cow, Dad!" Gary cried out. "Did you hear that? Do you really think that they will do away with the college deferment?"

"Yes, I could see that happening," said Carl Hamilton, knowing that his son had been born in 1953. "I heard Congressman Sam DeWine talking about it on the radio. There's a lot of anger over those college anti-war demonstrations."

"What am I going to do?"

"You were born in '53," said Carl calmly. "Your draft number won't be selected until February of 1972, after you are already in college."

As Carl mulled things over, the radio commentator continued.

> "In the Attorney General's office, lawyers are concerned about the upcoming ruling by the U.S. Supreme Court in the Swann v Charlotte-Mecklenburg decision, which examines the legitimacy of mandatory busing for racial integration. The Court will either let the practice stand or ban it.

> "In the world of sports, Columbus's own, golfer Jack Nicklaus, leads the PGA Championship by two strokes. Seems strange to be talking about this major tournament in February! But I guess a lot of things are a-changin' these days."

"Well, one option," Carl said, returning his attention to his son, "would be to sign up for ROTC when you get to college. It would allow you to finish college before you would be inducted. The war might be over by then."

Gary leaned back in his seat and exhaled slowly. *At least there's an option.*

"Dad, Coach gave a terrible motivational speech yesterday. Gino asked him to say something inspiring, and all he could mutter was, 'The league tournament is over; you're on your own.'"

"What did you expect him to say?"

"I don't know," said Gary. "Maybe how this is the end of the season, and perhaps time to think about winning and advancing…that kind of stuff. I'd thought he'd try to inspire us…like General Patton in the opening scene of that movie. You remember: 'I don't want to get any messages saying, 'I am holding my position.' We are not holding anything. We are advancing constantly. We are going through the Germans like crap through a goose.'"

"I remember…great movie!" Carl paused for a few seconds and then said, "Well, I think your coach is letting you find your own internal motivation. It's best if it comes from within."

"But Dad, remember Jim Bouton's book, *Ball Four*, and how he got his hand around that home run ball first, but another kid snatched it away a split second later?"

"Young Bouton learned how fierce his competition was. I bet it never happened again. That determination comes from within."

Carl looked out the passenger side window as they crossed the bridge over Hoover Reservoir. He was captivated by the passion of the early morning fishermen, already absorbed in their recreation. He felt the same way about his golf, and he wanted that for his son and wrestling. "How about this for motivation? Your mother and I will drive separate cars to the championship round. Your mother will bring Julia. If you win, you can have my car and take Julia out to dinner again."

"Now *that's* motivation!"

Gary punched the radio button for WCOL 1230 AM and raised the volume as Tina Turner began singing "Proud Mary." The song was ending just as Gary turned into the Worthington Monroe parking lot. He saw his teammates climbing into the school bus for the ride to Broadleaf High School. Gary parked the car and said goodbye to his dad. He was the last in line and had to settle for a seat in the middle of the bus.

As the wintry dawn gave way to a warmer morning, and the bus's heater kicked in, the distraction provided by the cold weather began to melt away. The emptiness in the stomachs of the Maverick wrestlers now demanded their attention, painting their mood as gray as the overcast skies. The Mavericks sat in silence…hungry, thirsty, and irritable if asked.

Gary looked out the window at the traffic going the opposite way. *I wonder who I'll draw in the first round,* he thought.

"I'm starving," moaned George "Gorgeous George" Bauchmire, the 119-pounder.

"Hey, Gary," whispered Mark "Marky" McKelvey, the team's other co-captain along with Gary, "Start something...or we'll have a busload of bellyachers."

*I think we already do,* Gary thought to himself.

"Hey Carlo! Tell us a joke," Gary suggested.

Carlo rose to the challenge. "Um...here's one you might like...it's a Little Johnny joke. On the first day of school, the third-grade teacher announced an icebreaker.

"'When it is your turn', she said, 'I want you to stand up and tell us your name, tell us your father's occupation, spell it, and then tell us something interesting. Marcy, you go first, and then Kevin, Reggie, and Johnny.

'My name is Marcy,' continued Carlo in his best imitation of a 10-year old school-girl, 'My daddy is a banker, b-a-n-k-e-r, and if he was here, he would give us each a shiny new penny.'

'My name is Kevin. My father is a baker, b-a-k-e-r, and if he was here today, he would give us a fresh-baked cookie.'

Reggie stood up. 'My name is Reggie, and my daddy is a 'lectrician. That's l-e-k-t-r-i-s-h-u-n ... no wait ... l-e-c-k-t-r-i-s-h-u-n ... no, that's wrong ... l-e-c-t-r-i-s-h—'

'My name is Johnny,' Little Johnny interrupted, 'and my daddy is a bookie, that's b-o-o-k-i-e, and he would give you 4-to-1 odds that Reggie ain't never gonna spell 'electrician!'"

Amid the howls of laughter, Coach Duke stood up from his seat and looked back at the team, his face red. "Carlo, that's *not* appropriate! Did you forget *already* what I said at the end of practice yesterday? Don't use 'Reggie.' Use another name if you ever tell that joke again."

"What?" protested Carlo.

"Carlo…think. The name Reggie, more often than not, will call up an image of Reggie Jackson. You're crossing the color line, Carlo," declared Coach Duke. "*Don't* cross that line. Ever again. Think how *others* might feel about what you say. No more jokes. Start thinking about the tournament."

The gray silence returned. *I've got to do something,* thought Gary. *A surly team will have no spirit for the matches. There would be no chance to reach the team goal—first place after the first round.*

"So, Gino," Gary said in a stage whisper, "do you think it helps to get motivated before a match?"

"Why wouldn't it?" Gino replied.

"I don't think every athletic endeavor is improved by hating or working up some type of rah-rah cheering."

"Give me an example."

"Hmm…say you are golfing, and you need to make a five-foot putt. I don't think a cheerleader would help. You need to concentrate. Same for a baseball player trying to hit a curveball."

"Yeah, but wrestling is more physical than golf or baseball," said Gino.

"Yes," said Gary, "you're right. Wrestling is the physical version of chess…except there's no requirement to alternate—to take turns. But, you still need to know all the moves and counters, like chess. You also need to keep your wits. If you push ahead fearlessly, you could get reckless and get pinned…which is like being checkmated in chess."

"Makes sense. You could get over-confident and make an overly aggressive move, which might play into your opponent's strength…like a trap. Unless I've wrestled the guy before, I have to get the feel of him at the beginning. But unlike chess, sometimes you need to make some split-second decisions out there on the mat."

"What do you do to get motivated?" asked Gary, a little louder.

"I think about how much I hate losing," Gino said with a laugh. "When I lose, I feel terrible the next day. So I fight to stay happy. I've been winning lately…so I feel great."

"You don't have hatred for your opponent?"

"I hate *losing*. I don't care who my opponent is, unless I've wrestled them before. Then, hatred of losing motivates me to focus on a plan for the re-match."

"I'll admit it," said Nic Stavroff, the Maverick 167-pounder, who was listening in. "I *do* try to build up hatred for my opponent. And it also works in football. I hate everyone and everything about that team. At the end of the game, I want them to feel tired and beaten. And I don't want to be friends afterwards."

Gary rolled his eyes. *Did he even mention winning?*

"For crying out loud, Nic! You don't hurt them on purpose, do you?" asked Gino.

"No, well…you know…injuries happen. They happen in football, wrestling, and even in golf! It's part of the game. I've been hurt; I've hurt others. It happens."

*That wasn't really an answer,* Gary thought.

"So, how long have you been doing that, Nic?" asked Gino.

"Just this year," Nic replied. "I saw an old John Wayne movie, *The Quiet Man*. The Duke is an American boxer…a prize fighter from the 1920s who moves to Ireland, argues with a redhead, and fights her brother. The Duke said that he couldn't fight unless he was mad enough to kill. So he won every fight."

"Yeah, I saw that movie, too," said Marky. "John Wayne's character killed an opponent in the ring and felt so bad about it that he quit boxing."

"That was just a movie! It wasn't real!" said Gary.

"It's real advice, and it works for me," Nic replied.

"You're not going to kill anybody today, are you Nic?" asked Carlo.

"Not planning to."

"But Nic," said Gary, "remember our freshman English class? 'I'd rather lose with honor than win by cheating.' Which philosopher was that? Greek or Roman?"

"I don't remember, but I do remember the Italian football coach who said, 'Winning isn't everything ... it's the *only* thing!'"

Nic smiled when his teammates cheered. "All sports have written and unwritten rules. A good hard tackle is part of football. And in some games, the referees lose control and the players become animals. It's chaos with no boundaries. Those are the games I love!"

"If winning is so important to you, then why don't you drop to 155?" asked Gino. "You could make that weight."

"Football is my priority, so I'm never going to lose weight. Football is my entry to college and my path to more grant, less loan."

"I use something similar," announced Bruce "Bulldog" Landers, the 155-pounder. "I envision my opponent trying to steal my girlfriend...and it *enrages* me." By the end, he was shaking his fist in the air and baring his teeth.

"That's logical, Bulldog. Cindy has had a lot of boyfriends and she has a reputation," teased Carlo.

"Pound sand, Carlo," snapped Bulldog. But as the team enjoyed Carlo's needle, his anger gave way. Seconds later, he joined the laughter.

"Okay, smart aleck, what gets you up, Carlo?" asked Bulldog.

"I envision my opponent trying to steal my beer!" quipped Carlo.

"Or wine," added Gino, keeping the laughter alive.

*I love this camaraderie! Great distraction!* thought Gary.

"So, Gary, what fires you up?" asked Carlo.

"Well, before a match, I envision my moves working on my opponent. It helps with my execution. But for motivation? I'm kind of lost."

"Gary's lost! Organize a search party! Find Gary!" Bulldog hollered, keeping the energy alive.

"Pound sand yourself, Bulldog," replied Gary.

"Wait a minute…wait a minute!" called Marky. "I know where Hambone was going with that story. I read the book *Psycho-Cybernetics*—"

"Psycho…what?" Carlo asked.

"Cybernetics, you dolt," said Marky. "Now listen. The author recommends envisioning your next move. I heard that Jack Nicklaus uses that technique before every shot."

"I heard that, too," said Gary.

"Well, of course," replied Marky. "*You* were the one who gave me the book…idiot!" The Mavericks roared their approval.

"Coach, get Hambone some food…he's losing his mind!" cried Bulldog. Several Mavericks slapped Bulldog on his shoulders in support.

"I wonder if Marky's vision thing would work for me?" asked Lonnie Williams, the team's 98-pounder, a sophomore struggling on first-string. "I get so nervous before a match that I want to puke."

"Try it…and if you don't puke, it's working!" Carlo answered, tousling Lonnie's hair.

"Or, if I could do like Flex…" said Lonnie. At the mention of his name, Wayne "Flex" Fleckman, the team's 145-pounder, turned away from the window.

"I mean I don't know if it motivates, but it sure is intimidating!" continued Lonnie. "The way Flex stretches himself into a pretzel, and walks on his hands all over the mat, ending up at the green starting point! And then…*the frozen stare.*"

"Hey, if you wanted to do what I do, you could," said Flex with a calm but jovial smile.

Flex's reply underplayed his natural talents: stretching and flexibility. Flex used them to complement his strength. He thought everyone should spend more time stretching.

"It would *really* be intimidating if a heavyweight could walk on his hands, right, Lennie?" asked Gino. The mental image brought the laughter back to the bus.

Lennie removed the earphones on his portable radio. "Walk on my hands?"

"How about a cartwheel or round-off back hand-spring?" scoffed Carlo.

"Those are things this heavyweight will never even *try*," declared Lennie. "I'll leave the floor exercises to Flex." Lennie smiled and reinserted his earphones.

Flex took the floor, standing in the aisle with his arms braced on the metal tops of the seats to either side. "When I'm staring at my opponent, I'm not trying to intimidate him…I'm looking through him to erase his soul. That way the match isn't personal. I focus on exceeding his energy."

Gary broke the silence of the boys contemplating Flex's mental energy. "Well, staring somebody down never worked for me."

"Well, of course not!" bellowed Nic. "A flyweight…staring at another flyweight? Hilarious!"

The upper weight classes burst out laughing at the caricature.

"I just try to blank out all of my thoughts," said George. "I just react...the way a third baseman relies on his reflexes to handle a hot grounder."

"Hey, Lennie, what do you do to get motivated?" Gary asked.

"I'm doing it right now—transistor radio. I love the hard driving rock stations... you know, QFM96 and REO Speedwagon. Avoid Donnie Osmond!"

"Yeah, "One Bad Apple" could put you to sleep," said Gary.

"Now Lennie," began Mike "Mikey" McKelvey, the 126-pounder, "are you gonna tell me that you're not upset at all the hazing from your opponent's fans? It doesn't make you angry?"

Lennie turned off his radio and wrapped up his earphones. "It's different for me. I'm so much bigger than my opponents that if I wanted to hurt them...well, I could."

Lennie quietly continued. "I've been a target since I first stepped on the mat. Because I'm big and fat, others hate me off the bat. They think I'm stupid. I fight that every day. I hear, 'Why don't you get in shape?' or, 'The sumo event is next door.' I just ignore it. This is going to sound different, but I want to meet my opponents when I can."

"I don't think you're going to make any new friends, today, Lennie. This is business," said Gino.

"You never know! But you're right. . .today is all about making districts. And I will, God willing," said Lennie. "Gino, about motivation...what I do is, instead of the stare down, I grin like a lunatic! It plays with their prejudices, and they scare themselves. They already think I'm stupid... and now they think I'm crazy!"

"So, Bobby, what motivates you?" asked Gary.

"Given his record, I'd say not much!" chirped Carlo.

Bobby turned his eyes away from the shopping center outside his window. "Sometimes my dad helps me get ready for a match. He boxes my headgear around and encourages me to fight hard… like he did in Korea. Well, it does get my juices flowing."

"So, I guess that would be external motivation," said Gary, analyzing the situation.

"Keep that up and you'll have internal injury issues…and I mean soon!" Bobby declared.

*Okay, Bobby, you win,* Gary thought. The team's laughter confirmed it. The merriment ended as the bus pulled onto the driveway leading to Broadleaf High School.

# Historical Snapshot 7-8:

................................................................................................

## Excerpted from the book: *Tigerland*, by Wil Haygood[69]

*"In 1971, the enrollment in the Columbus Public School District reached its all-time peak of 110,725. Columbus Board of Education and Columbus school officials were involved in a plan that...systematically orchestrated a violation of the 1954* Brown v Board of Education *desegregation decision. There was a pattern of building schools in segregated areas. The school board in place was vehemently opposed to busing.*

*The local African American newspaper,* The Call and Post, *accused the school system of backing 'a construction program covertly planned to continue, forever, racial segregation of Columbus schoolchildren.' Its black editor, Amos Lynch, a longtime Republican, usually adopted a reserved tone on his editorial page. But the school board had gotten his goat.*

*In June 1974, Republican William Saxbe, the U.S. Attorney General, and former U.S. Senator from Ohio, took advantage of the chaos within the Nixon presidency at the time and helped move the wheels to get Robert Duncan, a black attorney from Columbus, Ohio, an open federal judgeship. The U.S. Senate approved Duncan, making him the first black federal district court judge in Columbus.*

*In 1973, a lawsuit was filed in federal court to stop the Columbus Board of Education's building program because it was promoting segregation. Judge Robert Duncan was given the case, and he ruled in favor of the plaintiffs in* Penick v Columbus Board of Education, *saying:*

*'In Columbus, like many urban areas, there is often a substantial reciprocal effect between color of the school and the color of the neighborhood.it serves. The interaction of housing and the schools operates to promote segregation in each.'*

*On July 2, 1979, the U.S. Supreme Court handed down their decision in the case known as* <u>*Penick v Columbus Board of Education*</u>*. Judge Byron White, appointed by President John Kennedy in 1962, wrote the opinion for the High Court and said:*

'*The Columbus Public Schools were openly and intentionally segregated on the basis of race when* <u>*Brown v Board of Education*</u> *was decided in 1954. The Court has found that the Columbus Board never actively set out to dismantle the dual system. The Columbus Board even approved optional attendance zones, discontinuous attendance areas, and boundary changes which maintained the enhanced racial imbalance in the Columbus Public Schools.*'

The New York Times *wrote on its editorial page:* '*Columbus showed a pattern of segregative choice that the justices could not condone.*'"

## CHAPTER 8

★ ★ ★

## Rick Startles His Son

...........................................................................................................

### Ohio High School Interscholastic Federation (OHSIF) Sectional Wrestling Tournament

Columbus Broadleaf High School
Columbus, Ohio

...........................................................................................................

## Robert "Bobby" McCoy, Worthington Monroe 175-Pounder

THE MAVERICKS WERE the first team to arrive. They walked down the quiet, unfamiliar main hallway of Broadleaf High and, reaching the end, found themselves facing west into the length of the gymnasium, empty but for the four large wrestling mats covering the floor. Expansive glass windows ran above the stands and the adjoining alcoves on the north and south sides of the gym, casting soft, natural light from an overcast sky. Bobby McCoy entered the gym last, his spirit energized by the cheerful natural lighting, much preferred to a harsh spotlight in a nighttime gym shining down into his eyes.

The Maverick coaches left the team and kept going down the hall to talk with the tournament officials before the coaches' meeting. Bobby watched the team clowns—Gino, Gary, George, Mikey, and Carlo—pull off their street shoes, and run around on the empty mats to get the feel of each one. Three mats were lined up and down the length of the gymnasium; three colored squares in a row: medium blue, orange and the purple at the western end. There was a separate red mat for warming up in the far-right corner, abutting the far purple mat. The warm-up mat took a bite out of the seating capacity in the north stands.

Bobby smiled as he watched Marky step forward to take charge of his duties as the co-captain. Marky corralled his team, shouting, "Let's go guys! Let's get weighed in!"

By the time the Mavericks were exiting the gymnasium, the janitors arrived to shoo everybody out. As they walked down the hallway toward weigh-ins, Bobby spied 13 large paper pairing sheets taped on the hallway wall, the official bracket sheets for this tournament.

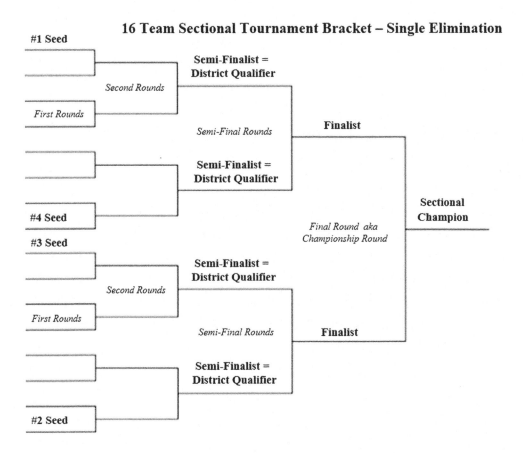

There was a bracket for each of the 13 weight classes. Each bracket showed 16 wrestlers competing in eight first-round matches. Alongside each wrestler's name was their school and season record. Their standing in the bracket defined their first-round opponent. Between each bracket line, there was a number, signifying their match number.

Each Maverick wrestler went to the bracket sheet for their weight class and found their opponent. Carlo was confused by the spelling of his opponent's last name and asked Gino for help pronouncing it.

"M-A-H-L-E-R? From Newark?" said Carlo, quizzically.

"Unbelievable, Carlo," replied Gino, "You drew the Newark Mauler!"

"Who'd you draw, Gino?" asked Carlo.

"Never heard of him. Losing record. Fresh meat," replied Gino.

Each Maverick found their first-round opponent and memorized his first-round match number.

"Game on!" declared Nic Stavroff as he put his finger near the bottom of the 167-pound bracket, Match 79. To Bobby, now next to him, he said, "I know this guy! Defensive safety on the Gahanna Lincoln football team. He tackled me hard…but it was always downfield in the secondary after a big gain. *We* won that game." Nic raised and flexed both biceps.

Bobby analyzed his pairing at the top of the 175-pound bracket. He was Match 81. His opponent was the #1 seed, Jackie James from Columbus Clintonville. His record was 15-0.

"Nic, did this guy play football? Have you heard of him?"

"Heard of him? Ha!" snorted Nic. "All-District halfback. But that doesn't mean he can wrestle!"

"Nice try. He's the #1 seed. That means he can," said Bobby.

"Yeah, he's a good football player. He leap-frogged me and pushed me down to Honorable Mention. I saw his older brother play football at Otterbein. Seemed like a regular guy. And, yes, he is black if you were wondering."

"Hey, don't worry about it, Bobby," said Gary, "that's better than hearing his older brother *wrestled* at Otterbein."

"At least you didn't draw Frank Schwartz, Jr.," said Bulldog, reminding Bobby of the wrestler who'd pinned him the previous week in the first round of the conference tournament. A shiver went down Bobby's spine. He wanted no part of a re-match. Frank was in the bottom half of the bracket, as far away as possible. *Whew!* A slow smile returned to Bobby's face.

"No way Frank would lose to Jackie," Nic said. "But we're never going to know, because you, Bobby McCoy, are going to beat Jackie in the first round!"

"Okay, guys! You've seen your first-round matches," thundered Marky. "Get your match number and let's find Coach Duke at the weigh-ins."

The main hallway was filling up with the multi-colored letter jackets of schools from all over central Ohio, including parochial schools, urban public schools, near and far suburban public schools, and a rural public school from nearby Licking County.

Everybody was nervous at the weigh-ins. The Mavericks all groaned inwardly and outwardly when Kenny, the Maverick 185-pounder, failed to make weight. It wasn't even close. When Kenny was nonchalant about it, Coach Duke grabbed his head as if keeping it from exploding. Everyone else made weight.

The hungry Mavericks made their way back to the team bus for a trip to the closest pancake house. The hungry wrestlers ate like it was a contest. At times, their jowls were so full that they looked like chipmunks.

At precisely the right time, Coach Duke reminded them about the dangers of over-eating and the time last season when one of their teammates coughed up his meal during his first-round match. The feast was soon over and the Mavericks returned to Broadleaf High School with their gym bags and dressed into their uniforms for the tournament.

The Mavericks gathered on the warm-up mat in the far alcove near the north stands. On the opposite side, the south side bleachers ran the length of the gymnasium between the alcoves. The crowd cheering for the Metro League schools and the parochial schools would gather there.

At a wrestling tournament like this, there was a lot of movement. No one had an assigned seat. Coaches would flit in and out of the doors on the east side of the gymnasium that separated the gym from the main hallway. There was little supervision of the wrestlers or the fans.

Bobby, standing next to Gino on the gym floor, watched Gino's friend, Jenny, as she picked her way through the crowd to join them and wish them both good luck. Cassie was there a few seconds later with her sparkle, her unique mixture of style and energy.

Bobby saw his father making his way down from the stands. Rick pulled Bobby off the warm-up mat and into a private conversation underneath the north bleachers, wanting to speak to his son in private.

"Do you realize who you're wrestling in your first match?" asked Rick.

"Yeah, he's the black football player from Clintonville."

"Don't let him beat you!" Rick commanded, boxing his son's headgear. "I've got good news. The union boss agreed to hold a spot for you in the apprenticeship program. Of course, you'll have to pass the test, but that I think you can handle. But you need to beat this guy to cement your position. We need to make a statement that we control who joins our union. That wrestler or one of his friends could be the one taking your slot."

The playful boxing grew in aggression. Bobby's ears were protected, but the emotional impact landed. Then Rick grabbed Bobby's warm-up jacket with both fists, shoving him hard against the back of the gymnasium wall.

"I told you last December," said Rick, his face reddening, "and I'm telling you again now…if you lose this match, don't bother coming home." Rick loosened his grip, smoothed his hands over Bobby's shoulders, and smiled a firm smile, confident he had properly motivated his son.

Rick left the gymnasium, allowing Bobby to reflect on the message. *I've got to win this match if I want to go home tonight,* Bobby realized.

The announcer for the public address system gave the opening introduction: "Good morning, wrestling fans. On behalf of the Ohio High School Interscholastic Federation, I would like to welcome you to the Class AA Sectional Wrestling Tournament at Broadleaf High School. We'll be starting in five minutes."

# The Ohio High School Interscholastic Federation

★ ★ ★ ★ ★ ★

## Central District Sectional Wrestling Tournament

Broadleaf High School Gymnasium,
Columbus, Ohio

★ ★ ★

# CHAPTER 9

★ ★ ★

## The 98-Pound Weakling

································································

### Sectional Tournament, First-Round Match

*98-Pound Weight Class*

································································

## Terry Duke, Head Coach, Worthington Monroe Mavericks Wrestling Team

THE PA SYSTEM announcer provided additional instructions: "Wrestlers, please clear Mats 1, 2, and 3. Scoring volunteers, report to your tables!"

With that, the wrestlers in the upper weights moved into the hallways outside the gymnasium, each team finding their own space. Many of the wrestlers in the lower weight classes moved to the warm-up mat. Some went back again to the cafeteria, where the wrestlers' moms had prepared a layout of oranges, apples, and bananas for their team's afternoon snack. The cafeteria was restricted to wrestlers and coaches only.

PA Announcer: "Coaches, please report to the Officials Table!"

Coach Duke joined his colleagues for a review of the rules, focusing on soft yet intricate interpretations for dangerous holds and stalling. Coach Duke always claimed he already knew it all, so he used the time to make new friends and refresh old ones.

PA Announcer: "Wrestlers, report to your mats. Match 1 to Mat 1, Match 2 to Mat 2 and Match 3 to Mat 3." The tournament had begun.

Coach Duke stood next to the folding chair placed in the corner of Mat 2 when Lawrence "Lonnie" Williams, the Maverick 98-pounder, walked onto the mat. His opponent and his coach were in the far corner, diagonally opposite. Coach Duke could understand why Lonnie was somewhat short on confidence. His opponents had dropped weight to make the 98-pound weight class, but Lonnie had not. As a result, Lonnie was usually wrestling someone bigger than him, and a few pounds of muscle mattered in the lowest weight class. Coach Duke decided to appeal to Lonnie's team spirit.

"You got a good draw, Lonnie," said Coach Duke. "Someone like yourself…unseeded and a sophomore. Fresh meat courtesy of Groveport High School. We need a team point from each weight class. You can win this!" Coach Duke looked Lonnie straight in the eyes. "The whole team is watching you. This is important for the team! Start us out right!"

Lonnie's breathing slowed down as he listened to Coach Duke. He moved to the center of Mat 2. As he was kneeling to put on the green ankle band, he closed his eyes and re-played in his mind his "go-to" takedown move, the far ankle pick.

Coach Duke watched Lonnie take his place across from the Groveport sophomore, who was wearing a dark red uniform with a star and a stripe. Both wrestlers assumed the neutral position for the start of the first period.

"Shake hands," commanded the referee.

"Ready? Wrestle!"

Lonnie and his opponent both went for collar tie and tie-up. After some arm fighting, Lonnie obtained a solid underhook with his left arm.

He slid his right hand from behind his opponent's neck and grabbed the left elbow, then pulled down hard. Fearing the pancake move, his opponent raised his torso.

Lonnie deftly shuffle-stepped to his left, and when his opponent's left foot came forward, Lonnie grabbed its ankle.

Pulling the ankle hard, Lonnie shoved his left shoulder into his opponent's torso …

… and drove him to the mat for a take-down.

It was just as Lonnie had visualized.

"Way to go, Lonnie," cheered Coach Duke.

"Two points, Green! Takedown!" called the referee. Lonnie was ahead, 2 – 0.

As the red wrestler hit the mat, he twisted onto his stomach to avoid giving up back points. Lonnie used his forehead and chest to apply weight and maintain control.

Lonnie maintained control for the rest of the first period.

*Phweet!* At the sound of the whistle ending the first period, Coach Duke stared at Lonnie and pumped his fist. Not needing a towel, water, or delay, Lonnie moved to the center circle for the coin flip to determine which wrestler would get first choice over starting position for the second period. Lonnie won the coin toss and chose the top position. The referee raised up his left arm which sported a green wrist band, signaling "Green Up."

When the whistle sounded, Lonnie used the arm chop, driving his opponent to the mat. Lonnie alternated half nelson and arm-bar efforts to turn his opponent onto his back. Lonnie wasn't close to turning the red wrestler but held him down with a dominating ride. For most of the second period, Lonnie kept him flat on the mat.

Coach Duke could see the strength of the red wrestler as he strained to push off the mat. Lonnie used his forehead to keep pressure on the back of the red wrestler's head. Coach Duke could feel Lonnie's inner voice screaming in desperation, recognizing the need to keep this brute down on the mat. Coach Duke was pleased that Lonnie kept inserting the half nelson, which looked like action to the referee, so no stalling warning was called. Toward the three-quarter mark of the second period, the red wrestler was able to get on all fours and execute rolling maneuvers. Lonnie followed his moves and stayed on him like a backpack.

*Phweet!* Lonnie had maintained control in the second period, and still led, 2 – 0. Lonnie rose to his feet and gently danced in place, keeping his arms and legs moving. If he stopped to rest, he would never regain the same energy level.

Wrestling crowds love a "donnybrook," a rambunctious yet evenly matched contest where the outcome could go either way…each contender wrestling move-to-move-to-move…and each scoring cleanly with few scrambles to slow the action, like eight-year old twins wrestling in the basement for their parents. Lonnie's match wasn't like that; the audience's eyes were elsewhere. It didn't matter to Coach Duke or Lonnie.

Coach Duke and Lonnie only paid attention to the scoreboard. Lonnie was ahead and the riding time clock showed over three minutes in his favor. One period left, with Lonnie starting in the down referee's position.

*Phweet!* Lonnie planted his left foot on the mat and stood up, but in a flash his opponent had his arms around Lonnie's waist and lifted him off the mat.

A wide-eyed Lonnie was dumped back on the mat with a hard return.

*Keep moving, Lonnie! That Groveport sophomore is strong enough to pin you, regardless of the score!* thought Coach Duke. He smiled as Lonnie kept moving next-to-next-to-next with stand-up after stand-up, suffering trips and hard mat returns. But Coach Duke's optimism soon turned to anger.

After another hard return to the mat, Coach Duke shouted, "Hey, ref! Watch the slam! Red is supposed to return my guy to the mat safely!"

The referee and his whistle stayed silent.

Finally, with about 20 seconds left, Lonnie was able to stand-up, break his opponent's waist hold by ripping the arms away, get hip separation, and turn around into the neutral position. Lonnie was ahead, 3 – 0. Both wrestlers were on their feet.

Lonnie went for the tie-up and shrugged his opponent away. When his opponent agreed to tie up again, Coach Duke knew Lonnie's opponent had quit.

As time expired, the scoreboard displayed, Green 3 – Red 0. The riding time clock displayed 1:45 of riding time advantage for Green, adding another point for Lonnie.

The final score was Lonnie 4 – Groveport Sophomore 0.

Lonnie stopped moving only when the referee raised his hand in victory. Lonnie was too tired to smile, so Coach Duke smiled for both of them.

"Great job! Great job!" shouted Coach Duke, pounding Lonnie on the back. "I'm so proud of you, Lonnie. Our first team point!" He handed Lonnie his warm-up jacket. "You won that one with your head and your heart."

Lonnie made a weak effort at a smile.

"I'm going to find Hambone. He's up next." With one more smile at Lonnie, Coach Duke commanded, "Go to the hallway and find your teammates. Tell them you scored the first team point…and tell them to behave!"

# CHAPTER 10

★ ★ ★

## Can Gary Gets His Act Together?

..............................................................................

**Sectional Tournament, First-Round Match,**

*105-Pound Weight Class*

..............................................................................

## Gary "Hambone" Hamilton, Co-captain, Worthington Monroe 105-Pounder

GARY WAS WAITING for his match in the hallway near the bracket sheets, talking with Gino, the Maverick 112-pounder and his frequent practice partner.

"So, Hambone, how about a little wager?" said Gino, grinning. "You pinned your next opponent last week in the conference tournament, right?"

"Yes," replied Gary, warily. "The guy from Reynoldsburg. I wrestled him in the first round. I took him down with my shrug-n-under and then pinned him in the first period. What did you have in mind?"

"Okay, so I challenge you to see which of us can pin our next opponent in the shortest time."

"That's not fair! You drew someone who hasn't won a match all season. A total fish."

"No, he's won one match and lost ten," countered Gino. "I have no idea how good he is. And you've already pinned your next guy. Remember when we were in our street clothes waiting for Lennie's match against that Westland football player? He was the one who came up and introduced himself."

"Kevin, right? He gave me a safety pin and told me to fasten it inside my letter jacket. I did. Said it was the first time he'd ever been pinned," said Gary.

"Don't believe him. I heard he'd been handing out safety pins all season!"

Gary laughed at Gino's conjecture. "Okay, Gino, you're on. Standard bet? A Wendy's double?" The teammates shook hands to seal their wager. During the regular season, when a dual match was held on a Saturday afternoon, Gary and Gino would go to Wendy's after the match for their weekly splurge. They remembered how good that Wendy's Double tasted after a week of dieting to make weight.

Coach Duke approached the two at a sturdy pace. "Hambone? Where've you been?"

"Right here, coach. Talking strategy with Gino."

"I thought you'd be on the warm-up mat. Your match is only three away. Let's go."

"Okay, Coach. I warmed up after weigh-ins. And I pinned this guy last week. Don't worry."

"I got my first gray hair last week, and it had your name on it," Coach Duke replied.

Coach Duke escorted his 105-pounder to the warm-up mat and discussed which takedown to use in the first period. Gary was confident his go-to move, the shrug-n-under, would work again, as it had the previous week.

PA Announcer: "Match 9 to Mat 3. Match 9 to Mat 3."

Gary moved to the center circle of the mat and fastened the green ankle band. He was confident, almost smug.

"Shake hands," commanded the referee. "Ready? Wrestle!"

Gary immediately secured a collar tie and tied-up with Kevin, his Reynoldsburg rival, but Kevin soon pushed away, wanting no part of the tie-up. Gary stubbornly pursued the same move.

Bout after bout of tough, aggressive hand fighting followed, until Kevin, the red wrestler, caught Gary momentarily off-balance, and shot his head underneath.

The red wrestler pushed his right arm forward between Gary's legs, the midpoint of the high crotch takedown.

Now completely off-balance, Gary fell forward.

Kevin stood up and then jumped on Gary's back, tackling him to the mat.

"Two points, Red! Takedown!" called the referee. Soon, the wrestlers rolled out of bounds. *Phweet!*

Gary sat on the edge of the mat, punching his fist into the mat. His go-to takedown move had failed him. The score was Gary 0 – Kevin 2. After the restart, Kevin maintained control for the rest of the first period.

Coach Duke looked at the riding time clock, determined that something was wrong. It now showed 75 seconds for red, the Reynoldsburg wrestler. Coach Duke took two steps toward the scorer's table and shouted, "Hey, Scorer! Watch that riding time. Turn it off when they roll out of bounds."

Gary unleashed a heavy sigh and shook his head in disgust. *How can I be losing to this guy?*

Kevin won the coin toss and chose down. Gary took the up position for the start of the second period.

*Phweet!* Gary had a difficult time holding back the red wrestler's energy. Kevin scored an escape with a powerful stand-up move, increasing his lead to Gary 0 – Kevin 3. Next, he lunged for Gary's left leg, shooting for a single leg takedown, head inside.

Gary countered with the whizzer.

Then, sidestepping to his right, Gary dragged his opponent along, pulling his opponent's right arm higher, off the leg, with each step.

Gary kept sidestepping to his right, waiting for his rival to reach up with his left arm.

When the red wrestler did, Gary was able to get an underhook.

Then, Gary whipped him over…

…and pancaked him to the mat.

Kevin landed on his back, but quickly bridged onto his neck and rolled through to his stomach.

"Two points, Green! Takedown!" called the referee.

"What about back points?" shouted Coach Duke. The referee crossed his hands across his body, signaling the red wrestler was safe; no back points were awarded to Gary. The score was Gary 2 – Kevin 3 with just under a minute left in the second period.

Gary tried to hold on in the up position, but Kevin broke his left arm free on a switch and scored the reversal. The score was now 2 – 5, Kevin leading. They soon rolled out of bounds, giving Gary a fresh restart. But Gary wasn't able to capitalize, and Kevin rode out the second period. A frown puckered the edges of Gary's normally amiable mouth as he sat on the edge of the mat, out of bounds and out of sorts.

"Hambone, wake up!" thundered Coach Terry Duke, throwing a towel at his wrestler. "I've got to visit the scorer's table. I think they let the riding time clock run for your opponent during an out of bounds. While I'm checking it out…*get your act together!*"

Coach Duke marched to the scorer's table to quarrel about riding time. The riding time clock showed two minutes and 25 seconds in favor of the Reynoldsburg wrestler.

Gary grabbed the towel and wiped away the perspiration on his forehead. From the corner of his eye, he spotted Kevin grinning in the far corner. A wrestling crowd notices when a #1 seed is getting beat, so the crowd was getting into this match, with foot stomping coming from the south stands. Gary punched the mat, as hard as he could. *Cheering against me?* Gary's blood rose in his temples, his determination returning.

He jumped to his feet and shook it off. Gary turned his head toward the north stands. He saw Bobby stand up and flash his hands. *Explode. Got it. Thanks, buddy,* thought Gary.

The fates had not entirely deserted Gary. He would start the final period in the down referee's position—which should allow him to score points. However, an escape and a takedown would only tie the score—and Kevin would win with riding time if the scoring sequence didn't happen soon enough.

Coach Duke marched back to his corner, shaking his head, unable to gain a reduction in Kevin's riding time advantage. But he did get the student volunteer, who was doing the best he could, replaced with a back-up referee. Catching Gary's eye, Coach Duke barked, "Gary! Get in there and put that kid on his back!"

Gary nodded. His coach was right. Gary returned to the center of the mat, taking the down position.

"Ready?" called the referee.

Kevin took the top position on Gary's left side.

As the referee raised his whistle, Gary moved aggressively, but early, to his right for an outside switch.

*Phweet! Phweet! Phweet!* blasted the referee's whistle. "False start!" called the referee. It was just a warning; no points were awarded. The score was still Gary 2 – Kevin 5.

Kevin scowled at Gary as both returned to their starting positions. For Gary, this was the moment.

*Phweet!* There was no false start.

Kevin went with a tight waist, far ankle countermove to block the anticipated outside switch. But Kevin's defense now worked to Gary's advantage.

Gary lifted his left knee and pulled his right leg under his left before Kevin could secure it.

Gary used his left elbow as leverage to pull his feet completely under and away. Gary was throwing an inside switch, a risky move that might give Kevin the opportunity to earn back points that would seal Kevin's victory.

But Gary was able to separate from Kevin, getting both his legs out. He continued to apply pressure with his left elbow, driving Kevin's head to the mat.

A split-second later, Gary was free of Kevin's left arm for a two-point reversal.

"Two points, Green! Reversal!" called the referee.

The score was Gary 4 – Kevin 5.

Even if Gary could ride out the third period, he could not earn a riding time point. But he could neutralize Kevin's riding time advantage.

Gary needed back points, so he pulled Kevin's left leg forward.

As Kevin struggled to get up on all fours, Gary allowed it, while pulling Kevin's head toward Kevin's knee.

Then, he reached deep between Kevin's legs with his right arm and grabbed his own left wrist to form a circle around his opponent's torso in a pinning move called the near side cradle.

Then, driving forward …

.... and falling briefly but danger-ously onto his own back, Gary rotated Kevin's shoulders onto the mat.

Gary scissored his legs to get off his own back and grabbed for a double wrist-lock, getting most of it.

If he could hold on for the rest of the match, he would score back points and the riding time advantage would be neutral-ized. If he could only hold on!

After a half-minute, Gary clenched his teeth to distract his attention from his throb-bing forearm muscles jumping under his skin. He forced himself to breathe. Only a lit-tle longer. As perspiration trickled into his right eye, he squinted to prevent its burning. He focused on his grip, the only thing holding the cradle together. When Kevin made a desperate effort to straighten his leg, Gary's grip was loosened to a finger lock. Gary rolled to position more weight on top of Kevin's leg to relieve his forearms and fingers. Gary closed his eyes, avoiding the clock.

His mind wandered to the day in practice when he had first learned this move. He remembered Coach Duke's advice, *"The best way to counter a cradle is don't get in one."* Gary repeated it over and over in his mind.

*Phweet!* The match was over. The riding time advantage for Kevin had been cut to less than a minute, so there would be no riding time points awarded to Kevin.

"Two points, Green, Predicament!" called the referee. Gary had literally held on for a 6 – 5 victory. He lay on the mat, massaging burning forearms with numb fingers.

"Wrestlers, get up!" called the referee. "Shake hands."

Gary put his hand out, and Kevin shook it half-heartedly. The referee signaled a Green victory, drawing cheers from the north stands.

When Gary looked back, Kevin was gone.

But Coach Duke was there, roaring with glee. "You snatched victory from the jaws of defeat, Hambone!"

Gary smiled and shook Coach Duke's hand. *No sense arguing with him when he's right!* thought Gary.

# CHAPTER 11

★ ★ ★

## Gino Lands a Fish

...............................................................................

Sectional Tournament, First-Round Match,

*112-Pound Weight Class*

...............................................................................

## Terry Duke, Head Coach, Worthington Monroe Mavericks Wrestling Team

COACH DUKE KNEW Gino, the Mavericks' 112-pounder, would be Match 21, so he had some spare time. He left Gary and the gymnasium to check up on his team and make sure they were behaving. Coach Duke found his assistant coach, Lloyd Bennett, at the bracket sheets, talking with Mike and Mark McKelvey, the brothers who wrestled at 126-pounds and 132-pounds, respectively. Over Assistant Coach Bennett's shoulder, Coach Duke spied the 98-pound sophomore wrestler from Groveport that Lonnie had just defeated. He was pleading with his coach to be allowed to go home.

"Just because you got your butt kicked doesn't mean you can leave early!" the Groveport coach stated firmly. "You'll wait…and leave with all your teammates!"

Coach Duke gave a twisted smile. He would save this story for the first day of practice in the fall. He would tell the whole story in front of the team and elevate Lonnie for a future leadership role.

As he looked further down the hallway, he spied Lonnie, Sparky, and most of the rest of his team having a good time. Reassured, Coach Duke returned to the gymnasium and found Gino standing on the edge of the warm-up. Standing to the side, Coach Duke watched Gary and Gino lock arms back-to-back, taking turns pulling each other off the mat and into the air, like putting on a backpack. Then Gino loosened up his neck with a series of neck bridges.

PA Announcer: "Match 21 to Mat 2, Match 21 to Mat 2."

"That's your match, Gino!" said Coach Duke. "Let's go!"

The coach and Gino walked onto the orange mat in the center of the gymnasium and into a corner where a chair was waiting. "Gino, this guy is a fish!" said Coach Duke. "First-year wrestler from Northland. Have some fun out there!"

Gino moved to the center of the mat, put on the green ankle band, and shook hands with his opponent, the Northland novice.

"Ready? Wrestle!" called the referee.

Gino sidestepped to his left, then tied-up, testing his opponent's strength and finding little.

Gino raised his left hand and wiggled his fingers just above his opponent's eyes. He circled around, and then did it with his right fingers.

When his opponent peeked, Gino reached straight across with his left hand and grabbed his rival's right wrist…

…and reached across with his right arm to hook his rival's right bicep for an arm drag takedown.

Gino pulled himself behind, but, with both still standing, his opponent windmilled his arm up and around for a whizzer.

Gino reached down with both hands and lifted his rival's right leg off the mat.

Gino pulled his rival around the mat, looking for an opening to trip him.

This made the red wrestler hop around on one leg in whatever direction Gino was dragging him. Through all the audience noise, Gino heard Jenny let out a whoop of laughter.

Gino used a left leg sweep to trip his rival to the mat.

"Two points, Green! Take-down!" Gino led, 2 – 0.

Gino moved on top and, finding Jenny in the stands, gave her a smile.

"Cut it out, Gino!" shouted Coach Duke, realizing that if Gino provoked the crowd, they could turn against the Mavericks. All the Mavericks. The Northland coach looked less than elated.

Gino allowed his opponent to get on all fours so he could go legs-in.

Gino inserted his leg, then reached across the Northland novice's back and grabbed his rival's far leg with both of his own arms.

Sitting backwards, Gino put his opponent's back to the mat and held it there.

"Two points, Green! Predicament!" called the referee.

*Phweet!* After the first period, Gino was ahead, Gino 4 – Red 0.

Gino won the coin toss and chose down, wanting to practice a special stand-up that Carlo had showed him.

In the down position, Gino bent his arms for room to maneuver. At the whistle, he straightened his arms to push off, pushing up while he leaned back into his opponent. He sprang off the mat hard enough to lift his knees off the mat and bring both feet forward and plant them underneath in one strong move. Gino was standing on his feet. The red wrestler grabbed Gino around the waist.

Less than five seconds later, Gino broke the wristlock, got hip separation, and twisted free. "One point, Green! Escape!" Gino led, 5 – 0.

Now that they were on their feet again, Gino's opponent reached for a collar tie.

Using his left hand to hook the other wrestler's right bicep…

…Gino lunged forward with his right leg and threw his right arm under his opponent's right knee …

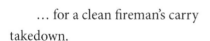

… for a clean fireman's carry takedown.

Gino finished the move by throwing his opponent on his back, never letting go of his right leg.

That prevented his rival from scissoring his legs and getting to his stomach.

Gino inserted the half nelson and lifted his elbow, pulling his opponent's head off the mat.

*Phweet!* The referee slapped the mat and raised his arm straight up, signaling a pin. Gino won the match...and a Wendy's Double from Gary!

The wrestlers unraveled, got to their feet, and shook hands.

The referee raised Gino's arm in victory.

"Way to go, Gino!" cried Jenny from the north stands.

"Gino," scolded Coach Duke, "Your hotdog display embarrassed the whole team."

"C'mon Coach! You were the one who said, 'Have some fun!'"

"Yeah, I said *'Have fun'*...not *'Put on a Flip Wilson comedy act!'*"

Gino caught the warm-up jacket thrown at him by Coach Duke. He pulled it on and bounded up the bleachers to join Jenny.

Coach Duke turned and walked away, massaging the middle of his forehead to prevent another wrinkle. He turned and headed toward the hallway, away from his team. After Gino's depressing display, he needed a break.

# CHAPTER 12

★ ★ ★

## Gorgeous George

...............................................................................................

### Sectional Tournament, First-Round Match,

*119-Pound Weight Class*

...............................................................................................

## Terry Duke, Head Coach, Worthington Monroe Mavericks Wrestling Team

**D**URING THE BREAK after Gino's debacle, Coach Duke's thoughts moved on to the next weight class, 119-pounds. He smiled and was instantly revitalized as he thought about his next wrestler, George Bauchmire. A natural talent. The only sophomore to be seeded. Did not need or want to be coached…and Coach Duke was fine with that. In the springtime, he was the assistant golf coach and he had met many high school golfers with the same demeanor. He let it be. After giving George insight into his opponent, he would sit back in his coach's chair and enjoy great wrestling from the best seat in the house.

George had been given his moniker "Gorgeous George" by his female friends for his coal-black hair and steel-blue eyes. They had all grown up cheering for a professional wrestler on TV with the same name.[70] Their allegiance transferred.

George's teammates—Gino, Gary and Bobby—were also in attendance, there to discern George's continuing progress. Plus, this could be the fourth team victory in a row for the Mavericks. With Gino's pin, the Mavericks had scored four team points in the first three matches! At this pace, the Mavericks were clearly on track to meet the goal set by Sparky.

PA Announcer: "Match 32 to Mat 2, Match 32 to Mat 2."

"George," said Coach Duke, "Coach Bennett says that your opponent is a junior from this high school with a break-even record. He's worthy. He'll probably start out in a low crouch. Be careful with that. Score first and take the home crowd out of it."

"Got it, Coach. I'll scope him out first," replied George.

As the match began, the two rivals circled the center, sidestepping counterclockwise. The Broadleaf junior maintained a low crouch. No tie-ups. Each would feign a shoot, and then step back. Not much action, but enough to avoid a stalling warning.

Midway through the period, George's rival shot straight for a single leg takedown. George blocked the left arm down and under, and then used a collar tie to pull his opponent's head down.

He used the reaction from the head throw to propel his torso counterclockwise and sprawled back and up with his feet.

His opponent's left arm, blocked low, could not grab an ankle.

Springing like a cat onto a sofa, George landed his chest in the middle of his opponent's back.

Maintaining his counterclockwise momentum, George moved around and behind his opponent cleanly in less than a second.

Anyone in the crowd who blinked would have missed George's go-behind takedown.

"Two points, Green," called the referee calmly, hiding his astonishment.

In a corner of the mat, Coach Duke sat up straight in his coaching chair. He admired George's talent, unfolding right before his eyes. That talent emerged from the challenges of the bigger McKelvey brothers in practice, every day a donnybrook.

On top, George grabbed the far ankle, working it to maintain control and eat the clock.

Toward the end of the period, his opponent launched an outside switch move.

But just before the other wrestler reached the halfway point, George threw a counter…but it was not clean… leaving a tangle of arms and legs.

The scramble for control was on!

However, each had a hold that prevented the other from advancing.

*Phweet!* "Stalemate!" No points, no penalty. The wrestlers would return to their last official position, which would place George back into the top referee's position. George still led, 2 – 0.

George glanced at the clock. Twelve seconds left. Both wrestlers returned to the center of the mat for a restart.

*Phweet!*

George arm-chopped his opponent to the mat, and once down, the red wrestler made no effort. The twelve seconds ran out.

*Phweet!* At the end of the first period. George was winning, 2 – 0.

George won the coin toss and chose down. At the whistle, George launched stand-up after stand-up, only to have his partially upright body pulled back to the mat. But his energy exceeded his opponent's. He got to his feet, and since he couldn't remove the arms around his waist, he secured them. Then he fell towards the mat, and rolled. At the right time, he threw his body perpendicular, separating their torsos. Escape!

"One point, Green! Escape!" called the referee. The score was George 3 – Red 0.

Both wrestlers stayed on their feet the rest of the second period. The red wrestler was hesitant to commit fully to any takedown move, fearing George's countermoves. The wrestlers traded efforts at reaching out to grab the other's wrist or reach under an arm for an underhook. Each would try the arm-drag takedown, neither effectively. Constant movement, intense hand fighting.

With the lead, George was content to hand fight and join in the tie-up, occasionally breaking off and sidestepping counterclockwise before re-engaging. George expected the losing wrestler to shoot first, and he was lying in wait. Time expired in the second period.

At the start of the third period, George started in the up position, also called the offensive position because the top wrestler is supposed to be going for a pin. George was seeking nothing less.

At the whistle, George flashed his strength, arm chopping his opponent to the mat and getting control of both of his rival's wrists.

Then, he gained control of the red wrestler's left arm with an arm bar… and did the same with his right arm.

When his opponent looked away, George tightened his arm bar holds.

George pushed him forward, using leverage with the arms to …

… put his opponent onto his back.

George pulled hard on his arm holds while pushing his back into the red wrestler.

*Phweet!* "Fall! Green wins!" called the referee.

Coach Duke jumped off his seat, shouting, "Two team points!"

But he became nonchalant as he approached George. *Don't over-coach this kid. If it ain't broke, don't fix it. Let it be,* Coach Duke thought.

"Nice match, George," Coach Duke said. "Any questions?"

Looking his coach straight in the eye, George said, "No, Coach," then finally allowed himself a smile.

Coach Duke smiled, too. He was happy to be the leader of the first four Maverick wrestlers…all wins, and two pins. His thoughts swirled with pride and excitement. Six team points! *We've got the lead in team points!*

# CHAPTER 13

★ ★ ★

## The Brothers

........................................................................

### Sectional Tournament, First-Round Match,

*126-Pound and 132-Pound Weight Classes*

........................................................................

## Mark "Marky" McKelvey, Co-captain, Worthington Monroe 132-Pounder

"**H**EY, I DESERVE some of the credit for those moves you threw out there, George! I let you practice them on me every day," said Mike "Mikey" McKelvey, grinning as George returned to the warm-up mat after his win. Mike was Mark's younger brother, up next for the Mavericks in the 126-pound weight class.

Marky, the 132-pounder, smiled as Mikey repeated the go-behind move on George.

"Yes, Mikey, indeed you do. You agreed to put out only 75% during practice, which allowed me to perfect the moves. Did you see how smoothly I executed that takedown?" asked George.

Mikey jumped to his feet and started dancing an Irsih jig, proud to have made such an impact on his teammate.

"But then again…I was only putting forth 50% of my effort!" laughed George. Marky threw his head back and roared. Mikey stopped dancing. As George walked away to join Gino and Bobby in the hallway, Mikey sat down on the mat, his arms around his knees. Mikey couldn't beat George in practice, even though he wrestled at a heavier weight. He would do better if he wrestled at 119, but he was holding his own at 126 against bigger opponents. And he was only a sophomore.

"Mikey," said Marky, "Get that sad look off shook off your face. Let's go talk with Coach. You're next."

They walked off the warm-up mat to where Coach Duke was standing. "Mikey," said Coach Duke, "we need this team point to stay on top. Take charge! You gotta believe!"

Marky disapproved of the approach. Marky thought Coach Duke was putting the team needs ahead of his brother's. When a wrestler takes the mat, it's a one-on-one match-up. Intensely personal. What moves would help his brother? Marky wanted to focus on that. The exhortation to be aggressive was okay, but Marky knew his brother could be reckless.

PA Announcer: "Match 38 to Mat 3, Match 38 to Mat 3."

Mikey and Coach Duke walked just a few steps between the red warm-up mat in the northwest corner and the coach's chair in the northwest corner of Mat 3, the purple mat centered on the far west side on the gym.

"Okay, Mikey," yelled Coach Duke, "Go get 'em!"

Mikey nodded, then headed for the center of the mat to complete the pre-match ritual. He secured the green band around his ankle as his teammates had.

Marky was joined in the north stands by Gary, George, and Bobby. No one knew where Carlo was.

"Shake hands," commanded the referee. "Ready? Wrestle!"

Mikey and the Central senior tied-up and broke off. They fought with their hands, trying to gain a favorable hold. They grabbed for collar ties, and when one of them got one, he pulled down as hard as he could, trying to create an opening. Good, clean, tough wrestling.

Mikey's opponent was the first to lunge forward, shooting for a double leg take-down. Mikey used his forearms to block his rival's shoulders and lifted his legs off the mat, easily sprawling away.

"Way to go, Mikey!" called Coach Duke.

There wasn't much other action, and the first period ended in a scoreless tie.

At the beginning of the second period, Mikey won the coin toss and chose down. He wanted to score first.

At the whistle, Mikey flexed his left bicep against the arm chop, leaned back into his opponent, and brought his left foot to the mat. The other wrestler used his right arm around Mikey's waist to lift him onto his feet, and then swept Mikey's leg with a refined move, tripping Mikey back to the mat.

On the way down to the mat, Mikey tucked his head into a beautifully executed granby roll and twisted away.

"One point, Green!"

Both wrestlers were now on their feet in the neutral position. Enjoying his lead, and feeling his oats, Mikey relaxed as he moved about. From the stands, Marky recognized a touch of swagger.

Mikey agreed to the offer when his opponent reached for a tie-up. Pulling down on the red wrestler's head with his right hand, Mikey muscled his way into an overhook with his left arm. His right arm went for an underhook.

When Mikey felt his underhook, he stepped back with his left leg and twisted the red wrestler like a rodeo cowboy bringing down a calf.

The Central senior did not cooperate.

As Mikey's overhook slipped down to his rival's elbow, Mikey found himself falling more than twisting.

Mikey's fearlessness had exceeded his better judgement!

The Central senior pushed forward, securing the takedown and putting Mikey on his back for two more back points.

"Two points, Red! Takedown, and Two points, Red! Predicament!" called the referee.

Mikey was now behind, 1 – 4.

Mikey rolled to his belly, getting off his back to avoid being pinned. But he never recovered from the first mistake.

His opponent stayed in the up position for the remainder of the second period, giving Mikey little opportunity to escape. In the third period, Mikey started on top as the offensive wrestler but could not score back points.

The final score was Mikey 1 – Central Senior 4.

After the post-match ritual, Mikey threw his hands in the air while shaking his head in disgust. Marky walked over to his brother and gave him his warm-up jacket. He was about to speak but stopped as Coach Duke approached.

"I'm proud that you took the fight to the senior. Initiative! God, I love it! Next year, Mikey, you'll be back and better than ever."

"I don't know if I'll be back. I hate losing," snapped Mikey. "I put in all this hard work and then this happens. I know I outworked that guy. I should have won that match."

"Mikey, hard work gives you confidence—not a guarantee! You know that! Tough loss. Shake it off. Forget about it." Coach Duke's stern rebuttal turned sly as he continued, "Besides, I have a story for you. I want to tell you about what Lonnie's opponent did after their match. I'll tell you the whole story on the first day of practice in the fall."

"What?!" asked Marky and Mikey in unison.

"I'm asking both of you for a favor," said Coach Duke. Now, pointing with both index fingers at the brothers, he continued, "At the first day of practice in the fall, I want you to remind me to tell a story about Lonnie's first-round opponent, the Groveport sophomore."

Mikey left to find Lonnie and try to solve the riddle. With Mikey gone, Coach Duke approached Marky. Assistant Coach Bennett joined in. The trio discussed Marky's opponent, a tall and lanky senior from Marion-Franklin, a Columbus city school. The crowd in the south stands would be cheering for their fellow city league wrestler.

"Don't let this guy get leverage on you," Coach Duke said with a note of finality.

PA Announcer: "Match 44 to Mat 1, Match 44 to Mat 1."

Marky stepped onto the blue mat, the closest mat to the entrance, on the east side of the gymnasium. The bleachers on each side of the mat, the south stands and the north stands, were full. As Marky was putting on his green ankle band, he tried to catch his opponent's eye, hoping for a stare down.

When the city league wrestler returned eye contact, Marky's eyes went wide. The guy was grinning! Marky lost his train of thought, and immediately felt off balance.

"Shake hands! Ready? Wrestle!"

Marky shook it off and started sidestepping to his left, clockwise. Again and again he avoided the tie-up that the red wrestler was reaching out for.

With perfect timing, Marky lunged just after his opponent raised his arm.

He then stepped forward with his right leg, driving hard into his opponent.

Reaching down with his right arm, Marky tripped the red wrestler's left leg.

Marky's takedown move was unorthodox—he shot his own style single leg with his head outside his opponent's toro. An uncommitted effort would have allowed the red wrestler to apply a crossface and whip Marky over onto his back.

"He who hesitates is lost!" Coach Duke said to anyone around him who was listening.

When the wrestlers landed on the mat, they scrambled for control. Marky inserted a half nelson, and his opponent curled his long torso away.

"Two points, Green! Takedown!" called the referee.

Marky rode out the rest of the first period and preserved his 2 – 0 lead.

Marky started the second period in the down position. At the whistle, his opponent grabbed the far ankle and prevented a switch. His opponent was strong on top and controlled Marky for most of the second period.

With 35 seconds left, Marky lurched his way through a stand-up escape, each step contested.

When he got to his feet, he turned into his opponent, pushed down on his opponent's arms wrapped around his waist, and used his hips to break the wristlock.

"One point, Green! Escape!" called the referee. Marky led 3 – 0.

With both wrestlers on their feet again in the neutral position, Marky resumed sidestepping to his left.

The Marion-Franklin wrestler executed a single leg takedown on Marky's left leg, head inside.

"Two points, Red! Takedown!"

Marky was still ahead, 3 – 2.

The second period ended with Marky in the down position. He would start the third period in the up position, still leading 3 – 2.

*Phweet!* Marky's opponent executed a stand-up and escape, which tied the score, 3 – 3. Both on their feet, Marky took a step forward with his right knee, offering it as bait to tempt his opponent into throwing a single leg takedown at Marky's right leg. But the Marion-Franklin team had been trained to avoid the bait, having full knowledge of the devastating chinn drop move.

The Marion-Franklin senior feigned for Marky's bait, but then swept around counterclockwise again with a single leg sweep, completing the takedown after a scramble.

"Two points, Red! Takedown!" called the referee.

Marky was losing 3 – 5. Fans in both the north and south stands were standing and shouting encouragement to their wrestler. The family members were standing and cheering the loudest.

Marky turned to his stomach when the scramble was over. He used a push-up to get his chest off the mat and then himself onto all fours. When the Marion-Franklin senior let go of Marky's left elbow to throw an arm chop, Marky started an outside switch, his left arm free.

The score was now tied, 5 – 5, with Marky in the top postion, on the right side of his opponent.

Marky needed back points for the win and decided to gamble with a gartrell roll. He used his right arm to put an arm bar on his opponent's right elbow, and then joined hands with his left hand coming up between his opponent's legs. Marky held the near leg and the near arm in a weak far-side cradle hold.

Marky threw his head and body over the top of his opponent's back, pulling his left hand off his opponent's right leg and onto the far leg. Marky purposefully went too far over and high on his opponent's back, making his head within easy reach of the red rival's left arm. The Marion-Franklin wrestler reached back and grabbed ahold around Marky neck - which was just what Marky wanted.

Marky pushed hard with both feet against the mat to start the roll.

Marky rolled onto his own back…

…and used the momentum to pull the red rival onto his back, and held him there for ten seconds.

"Three points, Green! Near Fall!" called the referee. Marky led, 8 – 5.

After ten seconds of wriggling, the Marion-Franklin senior broke Marky's finger hold and turned onto his stomach. He pulled his knees to his chest and got to all fours. He stood up and escaped, cutting Marky's lead to 8 – 6.

Marky knew his opponent had a strong sweep attack against his left leg, so he circled counterclockwise. The other direction would run into traffic. His opponent tried the sweep single over and over, but never got close. The clock ran out. The final score was Marky 8 – Marion-Franklin Senior 6.

The fans on both sides rose and gave both grapplers hearty applause.

"Nice match," said the Marion-Franklin senior, extending his hand while catching his breath. "What was that move you threw at the end? Some kind of trick?"

After the post-match ritual, the two wrestlers resumed their conversation as they walked into the hallway. About five minutes later, when they were finished, they shook hands in earnest, enjoying the singular bond that fellow wrestlers share.

Walking away, Marky thought, *He's a happy warrior…reminds me of Lee Trevino, the professional golfer who is always smiling, yet was the tour's leading money winner in 1970.*

Marky imagined another pro golfer trying to stare down Lee Trevino. That would never work. Marky made himself a promise to give up the stare down. He walked further down the hallway in search of his younger brother, but all he could see was Coach Duke, still searching the hallways for Carlo.

# CHAPTER 14

★ ★ ★

## Carlo Pays the Piper

........................................................................................

**Sectional Tournament, First-Round Match,**

*138-Pound Weight Class*

........................................................................................

## Carlo Rossini, Worthington Monroe 138-Pounder

CARLO HOPPED BACK and forth in the back corner of the red warm-up mat, crisscrossing his arms to generate blood flow. He was talking with Gino and they were all smiles, pleased with how well the team was doing. Five wins in the first six weight classes! It helped Carlo to know that the team was depending on him. It helped Carlo eliminate his distractions, to focus on a larger goal.

"There you are, Carlo!" said Coach Duke, a little breathless as he approached. "I've been wandering the halls looking for you!"

"Been right here, Coach. Getting ready!"

Coach Duke let go a sigh of relief. Carlo looked ready. "So, how ya feelin'?" asked Coach Duke.

"Feeling good, Coach," said Carlo, shooting a relaxed grin as he danced in place.

Carlo watched Coach Duke's shoulders relax as well. Coach Duke began offering instructions, "I just heard you and Gino calling him 'The Newark Mauler,' and that might be close. He looks like he's worked for years on a farm and has the strength to show for it! Don't try to muscle him…you have more experience. Heck, you were wrestling when you were in diapers! Use your wiles and your moves."

"Got it," Carlo said, continuing his warm-up dance.

PA Announcer: "Match 52 to Mat 3, Match 52 to Mat 3."

The two wrestlers put on their ankle bands and took the neutral position in the center of the mat. Carlo wore the green ankle band, like his teammates.

"Shake hands," called the referee.

Carlo reached out his hand and found his opponent giving him the death stare. Carlo shrugged it off.

"Ready? Wrestle!"

Carlo thought about using the shrug-and-under, so he joined in a tie-up with his opponent to feel things out. But the Newark Mauler did not hesitate. He used his left hand to hook Carlo's right elbow…then threw the other arm around Carlo's neck… and popped his right hip into Carlo's navel. It was an attempt at a throw takedown.

*I know this move!* Carlo thought. Assistant Coach Bennett had drilled the Mavericks on how to throw it…and counter it.

Carlo became dead weight. He fell to his knees…wrapped his arms around his opponent's waist…and pulled him down and sideways to his left.

The Newark Mauler held onto his headlock too long and allowed Carlo to bring him down. A few seconds later, the red wrestler was on his back, fighting Carlo's pinning move. The red wrestler struggled onto his belly, landing close to the outside circle on the mat.

*Phweet!* "Out of bounds!" the referee called, and the clock stopped. "Two points, Green, for the Takedown, and three points, Green, for the Near Fall." Carlo led 5 – 0.

The Newark coach raced to the scorer's table. "No way, ref!" he spit furiously. "They were both out of bounds! No points! You can't award points to a wrestler out of bounds!"

"They rolled out of bounds after Red rolled off of his back," called the referee calmly. "The points stand."

Carlo's opponent threw his arms in the air.

"Don't you dare give up," screamed the Newark coach. "You've got chores to do. Get busy. Score points."

"Wrestlers…Ready? *Phweet!*

Carlo slowed his opponent down with a double wrist lock, keeping the riding time clock running in his favor.

When his opponent finally broke free, he threw several escape moves. But Carlo went legs-in and rode the red wrestler like he was getting a piggy-back ride, maintaining control for the rest of the first period, still leading 5 – 0.

Carlo lost the coin toss, and his opponent chose the top position for the start of the second period.

*Phweet!*

From his down position, Carlo used the standard stand-up escape. He was raised his left arm in the air and planted his left foot firmly on the mat.

Then, getting to his feet, he tried to rip away at his opponent's arms, now in a handlock around his waist.

Suddenly, Carlo was lifted in the air and thrown down on the mat. The red wrestler had avoided a Potentially Dangerous call by first landing his knee on the mat and breaking Carlo's fall.

"Ref! Watch the mat return!" shouted Coach Duke, hoping for a warning call. The referee did not respond.

Carlo made repeated efforts to get back on his feet, each one a little less successful than before.

Carlo decided to crawl out of bounds, wanting a fresh start from the referee's position.

*Phweet!* "Out of bounds," called the referee. Then, raising his right hand with the green wristband, he continued, "Warning, Stalling Green!"

No points were awarded. It was still 5 – 0, Carlo leading. Still second period.

"Look alive out there, Carlo!" shouted Coach Duke. Carlo nodded and gasped for air as he crawled on hands and knees back to the center of the mat for the restart. His cigarette habit was catching up to him. Even though he hadn't smoked today, his previous cigarettes were now costing him.

To avoid another stalling call, Carlo had to move. And, being in the down position, he spent more energy trying to escape than his opponent did maintaining control, which his opponent did for the remainder of the second period.

After two periods, the score was Carlo 5 – Red 0.

Carlo walked to his corner and took a drink of water, taking time to rest. Each second was precious.

"C'mon…let's wrestle," called the referee, waving his arms at Carlo.

Carlo started the third period in the up position. His opponent threw the outside switch, and Carlo countered with his legs, but not cleanly. The scramble was on! After rolling around for a few seconds, the red wrestler was on top. But Carlo was holding onto his opponent's right leg, preventing his opponent from getting total control.

"Move up, Green!" called the referee, hinting that he thought Carlo was stalling again.

Carlo was underneath but still holding a leg and in technical control. *Move up? How? I'm hanging on for dear life here!*

His opponent's eyes pleaded for a stalemate…and a fresh restart.

*Phweet!* "Stalling Green, One point, Red!" called the referee. Carlo's lead had shrunk by a point, now 5 – 1.

When Carlo looked at the clock, he gave his head a slow shake. *A whole minute and a half left?*

At the whistle, the Newark Mauler stood up and ripped away Carlo's hold.

"One point, Red!"

The score was Carlo 5 – Red 2.

Both wrestlers were now on their feet. Carlo's opponent charged like a bull for a double leg takedown. Carlo swung out of the way with a single leg sweep, looking like a matador as he swept to the side and behind the red wrestler. Carlo grabbed his rival's leg as the Newark Mauler moved past—which tripped the red wrestler down to the mat.

"Two points, Green! Takedown!" called the referee. Carlo led 7 – 2.

"Way to go, Carlo!" yelled Coach Duke.

Once again, Carlo had a sizable lead. On top and in control. But he made no effort to advance toward a fall.

*Phweet!* "Stalling, Green!" the ref called. "One point, Red!" Then, glaring at Coach Duke, he announced, "The next stalling call will be for two points, and the one after that… disqualification!"

"For cryin' out loud, ref!" complained Coach Duke. "Just because you can't pin a guy doesn't mean you're stalling!" The score was now 7 – 3.

On the restart, Carlo's opponent threw the outside switch and scored a reversal. It was now 7 – 5, the Newark Mauler on top.

Carlo endured a smothering ride.

He caught a glimpse of the tabletop scoreboard and riding time clock next to it. The Newark Mauler was close to gaining a minute riding time advantage.

Carlo curled into a fetal position, shifting sides to turn his head away from the red wrestler's attempt to insert a half nelson. Finding himself close to the out of bounds line, Carlo soldier-crawled off the mat, rolled onto his back, and began gasping for air.

*Phweet!* "Out of bounds! Stalling, Green! Two points, Red!"

The score was now tied at 7 with 13 seconds left. Carlo's opponent had 50 seconds of riding time. If the Newark Mauler rode out the remaining time, he would earn one riding time point and the victory.

A hush came over the crowd as they sat frozen in their seats, wondering if Carlo could finish. All eyes were on Carlo, who was still laying on his back, gasping for air. No one moved, except Carlo's father, Rocco Rossini, who slowly rose to his feet to give his son final instructions.

"Hey, Carlo! Have another cigarette!" shouted Rocco. The crowd howled in laughter.

Carlo's face went red. He jumped up and marched back to the center of the mat for the restart, nostrils flaring.

*Phweet!*

Carlo leaned back and burst up and onto both feet in one move.

The launch confused his opponent …

… who hesitated…

… allowing Carlo to break away.

"One point, Green! Escape!"

*Phweet!* The remaining time expired. It was over.

While the coaches and the referee descended on the scorer's table for a review, the crowd descended into chaos…some booing Carlo for stalling, some cheering his victory, and some wanting to know what the heck just happened!

The referee returned to the center of the mat and raised Carlo's hand in victory.

The final score was Carlo 8 – Newark Mauler 7. Riding Time…Red 0:57, not enough for a riding time point.

Carlo stood alone in the middle of the mat and calmly raised his arms, relishing the cheers...and the jeers!

Carlo's vainglorious display was interrupted when his warm-up jacket was thrown at him by Coach Duke.

"Cut it out, Carlo!" commanded Coach Duke. "You'd think you just won the Olympics."

Carlo put on his warm-up jacket and, looking up, saw the look on Coach Duke's face. More than disappointment, Coach Duke's look included a warning, like he knew that Carlo's bad habits would catch up with him. Coach Duke would be right. This would be the last match that Carlo would ever win.

# CHAPTER 15

★ ★ ★

## Terry Duke's Firm Favorites

........................................................................................................

### Sectional Tournament, First-Round Match,

*145-Pound and 155-Pound Weight Classes*

........................................................................................................

## Terry Duke, Head Coach, Worthington Monroe Mavericks Wrestling Team

**A**FTER CARLO'S CLOSE win and show of bravado, Coach Duke needed another break. He left the loud gym and entered the just-as-loud hallway, crowded with wrestlers and fans. He headed for the cafeteria, the only area set aside for wrestlers and their coaches, where he surveyed the spread of afternoon snacks—mostly fruits and light snacks.

*Wrestlers eat too healthy,* thought Coach Duke. *No cookies anywhere!*

"I thought I might find you here," said Wayne "Flex" Fleckman, the Mavericks' 145-pounder, coming to Coach Duke's side. "I wanted to make sure you were okay… and see if I could bum a cigarette!"

Flex hit just the right button. Terry Duke cried out with a laugh, deep and hard, which released his tensions. Tears of laughter ran down his cheek. Flex's too.

"Not you!" Coach Duke pleaded, wiping his tears with his sleeve. He inhaled deeply and blew it out.

"Nah, I'm just messing with you," said Flex.

"That's good! Let's get down to business. We've won six of our first seven matches so far. With two pins, that's a total of eight points. We're tied for the lead in team points with Westerville. We need this victory from you to stay tied for…or maybe take the lead."

Coach Duke took a deep breath and paused. "Your next opponent is a sophomore from Whetstone, and his older brother wrestles in the 167-pound bracket. This is a trained wrestler, and that means he won't come at you with brute force at the whistle. There will be a feeling out period, probing for weakness. This is exactly your style. It will allow you to use your quickness and flexibility to leverage this guy."

Coach Duke and Flex moved from the cafeteria to the hallway doors just outside of the east entrance to the gymnasium, well-positioned for their planned entrance.

PA Announcer: "Match 61 to Mat 1, Match 61 to Mat 1."

Flex ran onto the nearby blue mat, un- zipped his warm-up jacket, and thew it to Coach Duke. Flex turned and bounded into a handstand, walking with artistry around the mat and finishing at the spot where the green ankle band was waiting—on the cen- ter circle across from the Whetstone soph- omore.

*A pretty good way to warm up the upper body muscles,* thought Coach Duke, with an admiring smile. The match came at a good time for Coach Duke. Flex's matches always brought forth a feeling of vitality in Coach Duke. Flex's wrestling style energized him.

"Shake hands," called the referee. "Ready? *Wrestle!*"

Coach Duke watched as Flex sidestepped to his left, circling the mat clockwise in a low crouch.

The Whetstone sophomore, dressed in white, leaned forward and reached for a collar tie with his left hand.

Flex latched onto his opponent's left elbow and threw his head under as he lunged forward, starting a fireman's carry takedown move.

*Good start,* thought Coach Duke, totally elated.

Flex's momentum carried him forward so that his left arm could reach behind his opponent's left knee, trapping it briefly on the mat.

For the finish, instead of picking him up off the mat, Flex just rolled his opponent to the side, which pinned his shoulder to the mat and brought his legs along for the ride.

Flex moved his head and chest directly on top of his rival's chest, forcing his rival's back to be exposed to the mat.

"Two points, Green! Takedown, Two points, Green, Predicament!"

Coach Duke was still smiling when the first period ended. Flex's opponent could not escape, so Flex led 4 – 0. At the start of the second period, Flex won the coin toss and chose up.

The Whetstone sophomore tried to switch, but Flex's ability to stretch prevented his rival from gaining control.

*Phweet!* "Stalemate!"

No points. Flex and his opponent returned to the center of the mat for a restart, with Flex again in the up position. He maintained control for the remainder of the period.

In the third period, Flex started in the down position and used the sit-out turn-in escape to slither away for a 5 – 0 lead.

Coach Duke stood up and took a step toward Flex, giving the thumbs-up sign, pleased with Flex's mastery. "Keep it up, Flex!"

Now, with both on their feet, Flex's low crouch continued to perplex his opponent. It prevented the double leg takedown because it would be impossible for his opponent to get that low for a shoot. Each wrestler took turns shooting for a single leg sweep. Flex was able to leap away like a cat from any arms and hands reaching for a hold. It was good cat-and-mouse wrestling. No tie-ups. A lot of action but neither pierced the other's defenses. The clock ran cleanly to the end of the third period.

The final score was Flex 7 – Red 0, with Flex earning two additional points for riding time.

After the match, the Whetstone sophomore gave Flex a token handshake and tromped off in frustration. *Flex has claimed another victim!* thought Coach Duke.

"I love your style, Flex," Coach Duke said. "Can I tell everyone I taught you?"

"Of course!" replied Flex, "That's what I tell them."

Terry Duke gave Flex his warm-up, and then stepped away for a moment of solitude in a corner of the busy gym. He stared at his fingers as he counted out the weight classes in order with eight fingers. Seven of them wins...plus two pins. Nine team points!

*We've got to be in the lead,* Coach Duke thought, feeling it in his bones. *The plan to have Sparky lead the cheer at the last practice worked better than expected. Probably because it came from a teammate.*

He weighed in his mind the upcoming matches. All the wrestlers were up against unseeded wrestlers except for Bobby. But the 185-pounder didn't make weight. Nine team points already...plus expected wins by Bulldog, the 155-pounder, and Nic, the 167-pounder, would make eleven points...and with Lennie a sure two points at heavyweight, a total of thirteen team points and the first-round team lead. *Thirteen points from thirteen weight classes. That's solid,* thought Coach Duke.

Coach Duke turned around and surveyed the gym. He bounced from foot to foot, warming up as if he were wrestling the next match himself. He would be. His next wrestler, Bruce "Bulldog" Landers, the 155-pounder, wrestled in Coach Duke's own style. This allowed the coach to act out each of Bulldog's moves himself, his body involuntarily moving one way, then the other, subtly following Bulldog's movements. After one more deep breath and exhale, Coach Duke spied Bulldog on the warm-up mat and walked toward him.

"Bulldog, you drew a senior from Bishop Hartley. His record is better than yours, but he hasn't been doing well lately. He didn't place last week in their league tournament, even after beating their league champion earlier in the year in a dual match. What does that tell you?"

Coach Duke and Bulldog looked at each other and nodded. They understood. When a wrestler reaches for a weight class that is too low, it can weaken him...especially late in the season. Coach Duke imagined the Hartley senior playing football at 175 and then clipping 20 pounds for wrestling...his determination to win overriding his common sense, his audacity superseding his perspicacity.

"We'll see who shows up today," said Bulldog.

PA Announcer: "Match 66 to Mat 3, Match 66 to Mat 3."

Bulldog stared down his opponent with his signature death stare, and the Bishop Hartley senior did the same. Coach Duke didn't see either blink.

At the start of the match, Bulldog went straight at his rival and tied-up. The Bishop Hartley senior was strong and agile on his feet.

As they broke the tie-up, Bulldog pushed away hard. When his opponent came forward again for another tie-up, Bulldog shot forward at a lower elevation, and then took an extra step forward, planting his left shoulder into the red wrestler's belly.

Bulldog wrapped his arms around his rival's legs, then arched his back as he took the next step forward.

*That's the way,* mouthed Coach Duke, arching his own back a little.

Bulldog lifted his opponent and dumped him on the mat. His opponent tried to counter by holding onto Bulldog's torso.

The scramble was on! Bulldog had not yet earned his takedown.

Coach Duke and Bulldog both reached back with their left arms and planted a crossface that broke the Bishop Hartley senior's finger lock. Then Bulldog moved behind and gained control.

"Two points, Green! Takedown!" called the referee.

Keeping his opponent on the mat, Bulldog forced his left arm under his opponent's left armpit and reached with his hand behind the neck for a half nelson. Bulldog maneuvered his body perpendicularly as he drove the half nelson forward, putting his opponent on his back.

Bulldog used his left arm to hold his opponent's head off the mat.

The referee blew his whistle and simultaneously slapped the mat. A first period pin!

After the referee raised Bulldog's hand in victory, Coach Duke gave him a bear hug, lifting Bulldog off the ground.

"A team point for the win and another for the pin! That's eleven total team points!" shouted Coach Duke. "And we've still got Nic and Lennie!" Coach Duke discounted Bobby's chances against the #1 seed.

*If Nic wins and Lennie pins, we'll have fourteen team points!* thought Coach Duke.

# CHAPTER 16

★ ★ ★

## Nic's Bad Decision

.........................................................................................

**Sectional Tournament, First-Round Match,**

*167-Pound Weight Class*

.........................................................................................

## Terry Duke, Head Coach, Worthington Monroe Mavericks Wrestling Coach

**A**FTER BULLDOG'S MATCH, Coach Duke had time for a break since Nic Stavrof, his 167-pounder, would be wrestling in Match 79, the seventh of eight matches in the 167-pound weight class. Bobby McCoy, the next Maverick wrestler, would be wrestling in Match 81, the first match in the 175-pound weight class.

Coach Duke spotted the problem. He approached Assistant Coach Bennett, and announced his plan, "Lloyd, I want you to stay with me for the first period of Nic's match, and then leave to get Bobby ready. Tell Gary and Marky to have Bobby waiting on the warm-up mat."

Then, turning toward his 167-pounder, Coach Duke asked, "Are you ready, Nic?

"Yessir!" replied Nic, "I know this guy from our football game against Gahanna last fall. He played safety, and made several tackles on me, but they were all downfield, after I had gained good yardage. *We* won that game! I own this guy."

In that football game, Nic had suffered punishing tackles from the Gahanna safety, but had gotten up smiling after each downfield hit, pleased with his 7-yard, 9-yard, 12-yard, and 15-yard gains. Nic believed that he was leading 1 – 0 in matchups against his opponent. Coach Duke could sense that Nic was taking this match personally. Nic was acting like one of Pavlov's dogs. ready to devour anything in front of him.

"Nic, Bobby's match is only two matches after yours," said Coach Duke. "Coach Bennett and I will both watch the first period of your match and then he will peel away for Bobby's." Nic nodded in agreement.

PA Announcer: "Match 79 to Mat 3, Match 79 to Mat 3."

"I got this, Coach. He's going down…*again*." Nic put on the green ankle band and his death stare, receiving an equal and opposite reaction from the Gahanna safety.

"Shake hands. Ready? Wrestle!" called the referee.

The wrestlers went after each other for a collar tie, bumping heads.

The referee let them continue, believing it was just an accident.

In their hand fighting, the Gahanna safety reached out for a collar tie and poked Nic in the eye.

*Phweet!* "Warning, Red! Dangerous move!"

The match stopped. A warning. No points awarded. Still 0 – 0.

Coach Duke motioned Nic to his coach's corner and gave him a fresh towel from Assistant Coach Bennett's gym bag. Nic dried his watering eye, checked his vison, and returned to combat.

Finally, the wrestling began, starting with hand fighting…pushing and grabbing with an arm or two, probing for an opening. When one or the other did get a dominant hold, it was not enough to overcome a football player's ability to stay on his feet.

The rivals used the entire mat…and then some.

*Phweet!* But the wrestlers kept fighting after moving out of bounds.

*Phweet! Phweet! PHWEET!*

The referee ran over and inserted himself between the wrestlers. After a stern look, the referee pointed them back to the center. It continued this way for the remainder of the period…tough, physical wrestling, close to being over-the-line, maybe sometimes over it. The first period ended in a scoreless tie.

When Nic lost the coin toss, his red rival chose the up position. Nic crawled on all fours into the down position.

At the whistle, the Gahanna safety jumped back and grabbed Nic's near ankle so Nic could not stand up.

But then his opponent kept pulling Nic's leg to the side!

"What's that?" shrieked Coach Duke, calling attention to the move.

*Phweet!* "One point, Green. Potentially Dangerous Hold."

Nic got up and walked it off, his squared jaw displaying the anger of any football player whose wheels were being messed with. Nic was winning, 1 – 0, but he was not happy.

The match resumed with Nic again assuming the down referee's position. The Gahanna safety was a formidable wrestler, a monster on top. He was giving Nic a hard and punishing ride, maintaining control and eating the clock.

When Nic was able to get on all fours, his opponent again grabbed Nic's ankle. Nic reached back to protect his leg, grabbing his own ankle.

This time, the Gahanna safety pulled up.

Reaching over Nic's neck, the Gahanna safety controlled Nic's head, and flipped Nic over and onto his back.

The Gahanna safety inserted the half nelson …

… going for the pin.

*Phweet!,* "End of the second period," called the referee. "No points."

"What?" spit the Gahanna coach, storming toward the referee. "He should get at least two points!"

"Time expired. The second period was over. No points," repeated the referee, looking at the scorer's table and getting confirmation. Nic was still ahead, 1 – 0, after two periods.

The Gahanna safety jumped to his feet, wild-eyed. The Gahanna coach gave him a bear hug from behind, holding him back. "Let it go! Save your energy."

Coach Duke instructed Assistant Coach Bennett to stay. "I need you here. This could get ugly."

The Gahanna safety regained his composure and crawled into the down referee's position for the start of the third period. Nic took the up position. Nic still held onto a 1-0 lead.

*Phweet!*

Nic's opponent went with the whistle, executing an outside switch in less than five seconds.

The score was Nic 1 – Red 2, the Gahanna safety now in the lead.

When Nic returned to all fours, his opponent jumped on Nic's back and went legs-in.

The Gahanna safety arched his back, leveraging his leg hold, and forced Nic to the mat on his stomach.

The Gahanna safety pushed Nic's head into the mat as hard as he could.

When Nic curled onto his right side…

…the Gahanna safety countered, reaching for a crossface, but landing a neck hold instead.

*Phweet!*

"One point, Green! Potentially Dangerous Hold!" called the referee. He then turned and pointed at the Gahanna coach, yelling, "And with the next call, Red will be penalized two points and then disqualified with a call after that! Any questions?"

The Gahanna coach did not argue, acknowledging his lost favor.

The score was Nic 2 – Red 2. Still early in the third period.

"Fresh start, Nic! Explode!" yelled Coach Duke.

Both wrestlers returned to the center of the mat for the restart, with Nic in the down referee's position.

At the whistle, Nic's stand-up was blocked when the red wrestler jumped on Nic's back, riding high, but using his weight to keep Nic's hands and arms on the mat.

Nic stretched his legs and locked them in place, trying to push himself onto his feet.

In the process, Nic's head came close to his knee.

The Gahanna safety made a circle with his arms, locking hands between Nic's legs.

Throwing his hips down toward the mat, the Gahanna safety forced both of them to roll as they hit the mat.

The rolling action provided the momentum to roll both wrestlers …

…first briefly onto the Gahanna safety's back…

…and then onto Nic's.

Nic's effort to thrust his legs in the air to break the hold only succeeded in rocking the cradle back and forth.

With each back-and-forth cycle, the Gahanna safety tightened his hold, like a ratchet.

That brought their heads so close that Nic could have kissed his opponent's forehead. But there was no love. Instead, Nic opened his mouth and sank his teeth into the Gahanna safety's forehead.

The referee did not witness the calamity since he was lying on the mat, focusing on Nic's shoulders and expecting a pin.

The screams of the Gahanna safety refocused the referee, and his eyes went wild at the sight of an offensive wrestler releasing a dominant hold and jumping to his feet… covering his forehead with both hands and screaming. When the referee got to his feet and pulled the Gahanna safety's hands away, he gagged.

The referee turned to Nic and pointed at Coach Duke. "Go to your corner!"

While the Gahanna coach held his wrestler and turned him away from Nic, the referee ran to the main table to find the public address announcer.

Two minutes later, a doctor was treating the wound.

The referee then visited the scorer's table. After conferring, he signaled a Flagrant Misconduct Call. Nic was disqualified.

Coach Duke handed Nic his warm-up jacket and commanded him to put it on as they walked off the mat. Assistant Coach Bennett followed.

Coach Duke spoke in a slow but firm voice to Assistant Coach Bennett. "Take him to the cafeteria. No one will be there until all the first-round matches are over. Tell Flex to get his gym bag and clothes. No shower. Get ready to leave. I'll join you as soon as I can. If I'm not there in ten minutes, leave anyways."

"Won't the officials want to talk with Nic?" asked Assistant Coach Bennett.

"I don't know, and I'm not going to ask," Coach Duke replied. "Leave now. Go! I need to pay the piper."

Looking around, Coach Duke spotted Gary and Mark with Bobby on the warm-up mat. "Bobby! Gary and Mark will take care of you until I return from the cafeteria."

Coach Duke then turned on his heel and went to take his lumps from the Gahanna coach.

"What kind of stupid are you teaching over there at Worthington Monroe? Come over here. Look at this!" the Gahanna coach screamed.

The Gahanna coach un-taped and lifted the gauze, allowing Coach Duke to see the truth.

"I've never seen anything so…so despicable in my entire career," said the referee, joining them.

"I'm sorry. I'm very sorry," said Coach Duke, looking them all in the eyes. "This isn't anything I condone. I assure you his wrestling days are over and—"

"This isn't the end of this!" roared the Gahanna coach. "I will report this to OHSIF. I hope they shut you and your whole program down!"

Coach Duke's face turned red, but he overrode his desire to argue back. He remained calm and declared, I won't challenge you on this…I will abide by whatever ruling is handed down. Thank you for showing me."

To the Gahanna safety, Coach Duke said, "I truly apologize. You didn't deserve this." He turned away and hurried to the cafeteria.

"This isn't the end of this!" repeated the Gahanna coach as Coach Duke left the gym to find Nic and Assistant Coach Bennett. He instructed his assistant coach to take Nic home immediately. By the time Coach Duke returned to the gymnasium, Bobby's match was already in progress.

# CHAPTER 17

★ ★ ★

## The Main Event, First and Second Periods

...........................................................................................

### Sectional Tournament, First-Round Match,

*175-Pound Weight Class*

...........................................................................................

## Robert "Bobby" McCoy, Worthington Monroe 175-Pounder

BOBBY WAS STANDING with Gary and Mark on the warm-up mat. All of them had witnessed Nic's bad decision. There was a strange silence amongst them, as if they were in shock. A strange mix of torments pulled Bobby in different directions. He was appalled at Nic, angry at the Gahanna wrestler for his provocations, and unable to turn back the clock to reverse the damage. He felt helpless, ready to lash out.

"I need to talk to Nic!" demanded Bobby.

"There's no time!" shouted Gary.

Bobby protested, but Mark cut him off, screaming, "You need to take care of yourself! You're up next, buddy!" The trio looked around. Neither coach was near.

Bobby's feeling of powerlessness turned his face turn red. His inability to solve the problem ignited an internal furnace. Adrenalin flowed as his temperature rose. He squared his jaw and looked left and right—looking for action.

PA Announcer: "Match 81 to Mat 2, Match 81 to Mat 2"

Bobby, Gary, and Mark stepped onto Mat 2, the orange mat in the center of the gymnasium. Gary and Mark stood in the coach's corner, watching as Bobby removed his warm-up jacket. The opposite corner was occupied by his Columbus Clintonville opponent, Jackie James, the #1 seed, and his coach.

## Jackie James, Columbus Clintonville 175-Pounder

In his corner on the orange mat, Jackie James was bouncing side-to-side on his feet while talking with his coach, Ed Lawson.

"Listen, Jackie," said Coach Lawson with a confident smile, "I just saw two Ohio State football coaches in the south stands. Let's put on a show for these guys. Your opponent is Bobby McCoy from Worthington Monroe. He has a losing record. Put him away early and save your energy."

Jackie nodded his confirmation and turned toward the center of the mat.

## Robert "Bobby" McCoy, Worthington Monroe 175-Pounder

Bobby threw his warm-up jacket on the empty chair where Coach Duke should have been sitting. Bobby looked across and saw Jackie's coach and his jovial expression.

Bobby's nostrils flared. *This is not a joke!* he thought. Bobby hurried to the center of the mat; his energy uncontrollable.

Above the buzzing crowd, Bobby could distinguish one voice crying out, "You can do it, Bobby!" It was Cassie, from the north stands.

Bobby grabbed the green ankle band, leaving Jackie the red one.

Bobby and Jackie were at the center of the mat.

"Shake hands. Ready? Wrestle!"

Bobby's pent-up energy and emotions were finally unleashed. At the whistle, he charged Jackie and pushed hard on his Jackie's shoulders. Jackie was forced to retreat, hopping backwards on both feet.

They began hand fighting and were soon in a tie-up. As they pushed and pulled each other around the mat, Bobby pushed in Jackie's elbow whenever he could.

Bobby's energy assured him that he would not be out-muscled. But he soon realized that he could not outmuscle Jackie, either. Bobby broke off and rejoined the tie-up several times.

The next time Bobby and Jackie tied up, Bobby pushed in on the elbow …

…and felt Jackie push back.

Bobby lifted Jackie's elbow, and it came up easily.

Bobby stepped forward with his left leg…

…and ducked his head under Jackie's right arm.

Bobby thrust his right shoulder into Jackie's chest and spun around clockwise.

As Jackie fell forward, Bobby dropped his right hand from behind Jackie's neck to around his waist.

Bobby was almost around and behind Jackie, but Jackie made a last-ditch effort to prevent the takedown by reaching back for a scramble.

It was a mistake!

When Bobby saw Jackie reach back, Bobby jumped into Jackie like he was his older brother, Dick, in a pile of autumn leaves.

Bobby pushed Jackie back, exposing his back to the mat. After a few seconds, Jackie scissored his legs and twisted his torso to get to his stomach.

As Jackie rolled off his back, he rolled out of bounds.

*Phweet!* "Out of bounds! Two points, Green, Takedown! Two points, Green, Predicament!" called the referee. The score was: Bobby 4 – Jackie 0. Still in the first period.

As both wrestlers returned to the center of the mat for a restart, the north stands cheered, and the south stands complained about the referee's call.

## Jackie James, Columbus Clintonville 175-Pounder

Jackie watched Coach Lawson leap to his feet, hollering at the referee, "That was a roll-through, Ref! There should be no back points!"

The referee turned and walked away.

*It's like being down two touchdowns,* Jackie thought. He stood up and shook his head and then his torso and legs, shaking away the bad memories and readying himself for the task ahead. He moved to the center of the mat and took the down referee's position.

At the whistle, Jackie executed an outside switch.

"Two points, Red!"

For the remainder of the first period, Jackie tried to put Bobby on his back, but couldn't.

Still, Jackie rode out the first period with a dominating ride.

At the end of the first period, the score was Bobby 4 – Jackie 2. Jackie won the coin toss and dealt Bobby the down position.

At the whistle, Bobby tried to rise up for a stand-up escape, but Jackie used an arm chop and a strong waist hold to pull him down to the mat.

Jackie applied a crossface to Bobby, then flexed his bicep to pull Bobby's head and shoulders back to the mat.

Jackie pushed Bobby across the orange mat and soon both wrestlers were out of bounds.

*Phweet!* "Out of bounds," *called the referee.* "Return to the center for the restart. Green down."

Jackie got up slowly and made for the center of the ring. He saw that Bobby's coach had returned and was giving him instructions. Jackie tried to read the coach's lips but couldn't.

*Phweet!*

Jackie arm chopped an elbow that Bobby was already tucking under. Jackie held onto Bobby's waist while Bobby threw his right leg up and forward.

Bobby tucked his head under and rolled across his shoulders which broke Jackie's hold.

Bobby had executed the granby roll to perfection.

"One point, Green! Escape!" called the referee. Bobby led, 5 – 2.

Jackie and Bobby got to their feet in the neutral position. They circled counter-clockwise, each looking for an opening. *I'm the one behind, now. It's up to me to press the matter. Let the thing be pressed!* Jackie thought.

Jackie lined up a double leg takedown and shot for it.

He failed to gain control when Bobby sprawled away and slid his hips down…

…breaking Jackie's finger lock.

*Phweet!* The second period ended, still 5 – 2, Jackie trailing.

# CHAPTER 18

★ ★ ★

## The Main Event, Third and Final Period

......................................................................................

### Jackie James, Columbus Clintonville 175-Pounder

AFTER FAILING TO get a takedown at the end of the second period, Jackie stood up quickly. With football scouts in the stands, this wrestling match affected his future. He walked directly to his coach's corner to set up a plan.

"Escape and go for another takedown. Avoid the tie-up!" said Coach Lawson.

"Got that," Jackie agreed.

The crowd buzzed, noticing a possible upset.

"Big third down play, Jackie," Coach Lawson said, tapping into Jackie's football confidence. "Your specialty. Be Jim Brown."

Jackie took the down position, trailing 5 – 2. He repeated in his mind the three crucial steps in his stand-up escape: *Left foot on mat...arch back to lean back...left arm in the air!* What his mind could conceive, his body would achieve.

*Phweet!*

Jackie pulled his left leg off the mat and planted his foot while leaning back.

Jackie's left arm reacted instinctively to block Bobby's left hand as his right hand did the same, preventing them from locking around his own waist.

Jackie brought his right leg off the mat, moving it forward to establish a strong base, and then stepped forward with his left leg.

Bobby tried to trip Jackie, but Jackie's balance kept him on his feet.

Jackie took two steps forward to separate his hips from Bobby's…

…and turned around to complete the stand-up escape.

"One point, Red! Escape!"

The score was: Bobby 5 – Jackie 3.

Jackie realized that he was near the edge of the mat, so he sidestepped to his right and away from Bobby and the out of bounds line, moving in a circular path toward the center of the mat.

"He's stalling," said Bobby's coach, more wishful than assertive.

As Jackie continued sidestepping around and toward the center, he stole a glance at the source of that preposterous idea. Jackie knew he was still down two points. *I'm not stalling. Don't believe me? Just watch!* thought Jackie.

As Jackie circled into the center, Bobby followed in pursuit. Jackie had finally coaxed Bobby into moving toward him.

Jackie stepped forward and lowered his head, shooting for a double leg takedown.

Bobby's forward momentum made it impossible for him to sprawl away.

Jackie made a football tackle on the torso and drove Bobby straight back and to the mat.

Jackie inserted the half nelson to prevent Bobby from turning onto his stomach.

"Two points, Red! Takedown!" The score was tied at five, but Jackie wanted more.

Jackie's singular focus was driving the half nelson forward, taking his opponent's shoulders to the mat.

Jackie held Bobby there for a few seconds, but then Bobby rolled toward his right side and scissored his legs to roll with the pressure. Bobby was able to move onto his stomach.

"Two points, Red! Predicament!" Jackie took his first lead! The score was Bobby 5 – Jackie 7, halfway into the third period. Jackie had taken his first lead!

The fans in the south stands leapt to their feet, cheering and stomping, rattling the wooden bleachers! The fans in the north stands rose and shouted out for Bobby. The uproar would maintain for the duration of the match.

Jackie wanted to put his opponent away; more back points would do it. Jackie saw an opening and committed to the far side cradle.

But Jackie over-committed and landed too high on Bobby's back, allowing Bobby to reach back and hook Jackie's left leg.

Before Jackie could lock hands, Bobby rose to his feet and bucked Jackie like a horse tossing its rider.

Jackie landed on his side, and Bobby jumped on top, pushing Jackie's back to the mat.

Now all the wooden bleachers rattled! Fans were screaming from all directions in support of two wrestlers entangled in a donnybrook.

"Two points, Green, Reversal!" The match was tied at 7.

Jackie was being held by Bobby on his side at just under a 45-degree angle. Jackie slowly raised his near shoulder, and then he rolled away. But not soon enough.

"Two points, Green! Predicament!" The score was Bobby 9 – Jackie 7.

"You're behind two points, Jackie!" Coach Lawson roared. "You need a reversal! A stand-up escape won't do it!"

Jackie caught the coded message and moved directly to all fours.

Then, to Bobby's surprise, Jackie leaned back and stood up. *So far, so good,* thought Jackie.

With both on their feet, Jackie felt his opponent trying to push him straight out of bounds.

Feeling his opponent's right arm around his waist, Jackie reached back with his own right hand…

… and threw the standing switch at Bobby.

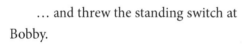

Bobby fell forward, and Jackie moved cleanly behind him.

"Two points, Red! Reversal!" called the referee.

The score was tied at nine with less than a minute remaining. *How can I control this slippery guy? Legs in,* decided Jackie.

## Robert "Bobby" McCoy, Worthington Monroe 175-Pounder

Bobby had keen radar for when an opponent's legs were being forced on him. He had suffered when Nic managed to get legs-in on him in practice. And now Jackie was trying the same.

*No way I'm gonna let that happen!* Bobby vowed.

His hand caught Jackie's ankle be-fore Jackie could get his first leg in. Bobby felt Jackie's half nelson, so Bob-by fell to that side and disabled it. The scramble was on!

Bobby worked his left arm free from the half nelson. It joined it with right arm, both now under Jackie's left leg. *Push out the leg and twist away,* Bobby thought.

His father was standing just off the mat—not a place he should be. Although Coach Duke was also shouting instructions, it was his father's voice that Bobby heard.

"Keep it up, son!" screamed Rick McCoy. "Show him no mercy. Do whatever it takes! Put him away!"

Bobby heard Jackie trying to suppress pain, and the referee heard it, too.

Bobby stopped, realizing that he was pushing Jackie's left leg in a direction that neither God nor evolution had ever intended.

*Phweet!* "Potentially Dangerous Hold!" Green!" A warning call against Bobby. No points. Still tied, 9 – 9.

Jackie got up using his right leg, holding his left foot off the mat. As he gingerly put weight on his left leg, the referee bit his fist. All eyes watched as Jackie took his first step, a limp. Everyone held their breath for the next…more graceful. A collective sigh was released when Jackie returned to his natural movement, walking without a hitch. The crowd in both stands offered warm applause.

"You didn't do it!" Rick cried in frustration, believing Bobby had lost an opportunity to win the match. Bobby knew his father was wrong.

The referee looked at Coach Lawson, who nodded, suggesting things were back on track. Jackie was bouncing into the air, raising his knees higher and higher with each bound. After several bounds, Jackie stopped and gave the thumbs up sign.

Near the other corner, Coach Duke caught Bobby's eye and snarled softly, "Sit out."

As Bobby crawled toward the down referee's position, he shuddered at the remembrance of how often Nic would pull him on his back when he tried to sit out. It was hard to surprise a practice partner who knew the counter.

Bobby remembered and recited in his head the key part of the move: *Throw the legs long.*

The referee signaled the rivals to take their places in the referee's position for the restart. The score was tied at 9 with 28 seconds left. Bobby would start from the down referee's position.

*Phweet!*

Bobby leaned against his left arm and raised his right knee so he could swing his left leg forward.

Jackie moved to grab the far ankle and found it out of action. Jackie responded by reaching under Bobby's shoulders.

Bobby's right leg joined the swing. *I hope I'm throwing them long enough!*

Jackie reached his right hand for a hold on Bobby's chin...*but missed!*

Bobby slid onto his left hip...

... and kicked his right leg over.

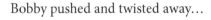

Bobby pushed and twisted away...

...until he broke free.

"One point, Green! Escape!" called the referee.

Bobby had the lead again, 10 – 9. Twenty-four seconds left.

The rivals scrambled to their feet. As soon as Bobby was standing, Jackie shot straight at Bobby's left leg for a single leg takedown.

Jackie pierced Bobby's defenses and raised Bobby's left leg in the air. Bobby stayed upright, hopping backward on his right foot and holding onto Jackie's arm.

Jackie swung a leg to trip Bobby, but Bobby hopped over it. Their momentum carried Bobby's right foot out of bounds in front of the scorer's table.

*Phweet!* "Out of bounds!"

The referee dropped his whistle, foreseeing a potential catastrophe unfolding before him. He sprinted to the scorer's table to prevent the wrestlers from crashing into it.

Bobby's eyes went wide as he turned and looked. Jackie was in position to launch Bobby over the table, but Jackie rapid-stepped to decelerate. He set Bobby's right leg down, turned, and walked away. They were inches from the table.

The score remained Bobby 10 – Jackie 9. Sixteen seconds left.

The rivals were on their feet in the neutral position, standing across the center circle, breathing deeply.

Bobby knew the double leg takedown was coming. But knowing that and stopping it were two different things!

*Phweet!*

Jackie charged before Bobby could sprawl. Jackie lifted Bobby off the mat.

Bobby had only one option. He put his arms around Jackie's torso and held on for dear life!

As Jackie stood up, he lifted Bobby upside down.

Although the crowd noise was at its feverous height, Bobby could still hear Cassie screaming, "Hang on, Bobby!" So he did.

The referee could not award a takedown because Jackie did not have control...because Bobby's arms were around Jackie's waist.

*Phweet!* Third period time expired. The match was over.

The referee raced to the wrestlers and threw his arms around their torsos in a bear hug to ensure that Bobby wouldn't be dropped on his head. As the rivals disentangled, they surveyed the crowd, both sides now on their feet cheering, shouting, and pointing at one wrestler, or the other, or the scorer's table.

"Way to go, Bobby!" shouted Rick McCoy. "I knew you could do it!"

"Wrestlers! Go to your corners!" the referee commanded. "I will confer with your coaches at the scorer's table."

The coaches were already at the scorer's table, where the tabletop scoreboard displayed Green 10 – Red 9. Time 0:00. The referee ordered a review of the scoring. Green 10 – Red 9 was confirmed. But that wasn't the end of it.

"And now let's look at riding time," the referee said to the head scorer. The riding time clock showed two minutes and 25 seconds for Red.

"Two points, Red! Riding Time!" called the referee.

The head scorer instructed his timer to update the tabletop scoreboard. The red lights displayed 9, then 10, and then 11.

"Final score…Green 10…Red 11. Red wins!" shouted the referee as loud as he could.

"What happened?" screamed Rick.

"Look! Look at the scorer's table!" came a cry from a fan of Jackie in the south stands.

"Did Jackie win?" asked another nearby fan.

"Yes! Yes! Yes!" came the reply from many.

"'Leven – ten, Jackie wins! 'Leven – ten, Jackie wins!" cried another Jackie fan.

The two coaches shook hands, nodding in agreement. There was nothing Coach Duke could do. Jackie had won the match fair and square, earning his final two points for having two minutes more riding time than Bobby.

The crowd shushed itself, casting their eyes on the post-match arm-raising ritual for official confirmation.

Returning to the center of the mat, the referee commanded, "Shake hands."

Bobby and Jackie clasped limp hands, both depleted by the donnybrook. The referee raised Jackie's right arm in the air. The south stands thundered their approval. The wrestlers were too tired to even raise their eyes at each other, so they turned and walked away.

"That's not fair!" Rick McCoy shrieked, accosting the referee.

"Fans belong in the stands...*now!*" declared the referee.

Rick threw his hands in the air and walked out of the gymnasium.

"Where's *that* been all year?" asked Coach Duke as Bobby walked by, taking his warm-up jacket off the coach's chair.

At the edge of the mat, Mark patted Bobby on the shoulder and said, "Bobby, you were *so close* to an incredible upset!"

"Close never counts," snarled Bobby, as he continued walking away.

"But Bobby! You should feel proud of that effort!" suggested Gary.

"Don't tell me how I should feel!"

"Hey! We were just trying to help!" responded Mark.

"Well, you're not." said Bobby, leaving the gym.

Bobby walked into the hallway, looking for a secluded nook to sort out his feelings. He needed to figure out which ones were righteous, and which were not.

# CHAPTER 19

★ ★ ★

## The Unexpected Conversation

..............................................................................................

### Robert "Bobby" McCoy, Worthington Monroe 175-Pounder

INSIDE THE HALLWAY, Bobby made himself inconspicuous amid the commotion. He found a corner down a side hall and, for the moment, was able to avoid human contact. Taking deep breaths and exhaling slowly, he closed his eyes and let his mind go. *Don't think, just feel.* Every nerve ending was firing, his entire body alert.

Hearing footsteps approaching, Bobby turned to find his mother and Cassie in front of him.

"I'm sorry," he said, "I let you down. I let everybody down," said Bobby, "I really –"

"That's *nonsense!*" contradicted his mother. "Did you hear the crowd? It was the most exciting match of the tournament!"

"Of the *year!*" said Cassie, "You outscored him…he only won with stupid riding time."

Cassie stepped in close, threw her arms around Bobby and gave him a big kiss on the lips, as if his mother wasn't there. Bobby's eyes went wide, but when he saw his mother smile and look away, he refocused his attention.

"Looks like you two are ready to leave," said Georgia McCoy, "if you'd like?"

"Can't yet," replied Bobby, coming up for air as Cassie giggled. "It's almost noon, and we're still in the first round. I've got to stay until the end of the third round. And soon, Lennie's match will be coming up. I'm going to find my teammates and watch it with them. After that, I'll take a shower and join you in the north stands."

Bobby smiled as he looked back and forth between the two women. "Thanks for your support. I appreciate it."

As Bobby walked back into the gymnasium and then onto the warm-up mat, his teammates gathered around and pounded him on the back. Bobby couldn't remember anything about the match, but as he listened to his teammates talk about it, his spirit lifted, reimagining it from their recollections. Then it was time to focus on Lennie.

PA Announcer: "Match 104 to Mat 2. Match 104 to Mat 2. Match 104 is the final match of Round 1."

As Lennie walked onto the mat, the Mavericks climbed into empty seats in the first two rows of the north stands.

"I know Westerville has 13 points in the first round," said Bulldog.

"And with your pin, we have 11 ourselves," said Bobby. "If Lennie gets a pin, we share a first-place tie for the team point lead."

Lennie didn't disappoint. He pinned his opponent in just 26 seconds. The Mavericks leapt to their feet and exploded with excitement. For the first time ever, the Worthington Monroe Maverick wrestling team was in first place at a tournament, even if it was a tie, even if it was just the first round. Sparky had established it as their team goal and they met it.

PA Announcer: "Attention, wrestling fans! There will be a short break between the first and second rounds. Please note that the food in the cafeteria is for wrestlers only. For visitors, family, and fans, the concession stands are open! In fifteen minutes, we'll return with Match 105."

With that announcement, most of the Mavericks left for the cafeteria, except for Gary, who was stretching to stay loose, and Bobby, avoiding the crowded locker room. Although sitting next to each other, their minds were miles apart. Bobby sat on the mat with his arms around his knees, enjoying his reverie.

Bobby looked up out of the corner of his eye and did a double take. It was the face of Jackie James, standing beside him…and then sitting down…next to Bobby! Gary was still just a few feet away.

"Only five wins?" protested Jackie. "When I first saw the bracket and your record, I thought I'd have an easy first-round match! But you were tougher than my opponent at my conference finals!"

Jackie continued, "You know, I'll admit it. Without riding time, you won that match. Just don't tell anyone I ever told you so. That's for you, only." Jackie chuckled. "What got into you?"

"I—I—I guess it was my mom and girlfriend sitting next to each other in the stands, watching me together for the first time," Bobby stammered.

"Wow! I didn't know a girlfriend could be so motivating. Maybe I should get one!"

"That's why I went out for wrestling, to toughen up and get into shape, which also helps in the girlfriend department," said Bobby, grinning. "What about you?"

"Wrestling improves my balance, which helps for football," Jackie said. "And, without wrestling, I'd be eating so many peppermint patties and gaining so much weight, I'd be playing offensive line instead of halfback. And that would make it even more difficult to date a cheerleader."

"Dating a cheerleader…the bond that unites all guys," said Gary. The trio shared a chuckle and introduced themselves.

"My father is pushing me to get into better shape through wrestling," Bobby said. "He's a plumber, and when I help him, I'd *better* keep up. It's the only way to avoid harassment. And when those union guys start dishing it out, it can get brutal."

"So, your pops is in the plumber's union?" asked Jackie.

"Yeah, he's a long-time member with a lot of seniority. He's pushing me to get in shape so he can recommend me for their apprentice program."

"Nice! My pops has a friend, Isaiah, who's in that union. My practice partner would like to enter that same program, but Isaiah says he has no pull. Last school year, a guy came to our high school and said there's an entrance test and anyone who passes can become an apprentice. But apparently that's not true. At least not true for everyone. But it's all tied up in the courts."

*There's another side to this story! His practice partner might want to be a plumber more than I do,* thought Bobby.

"Well—um—my dad tells me it's not easy getting in, even for me. I'm not guaranteed a slot, either," said Bobby, backpedaling. "And I'm not sure that's what I want anyways."

"Well, what *do* you want to do?" asked Jackie.

Gary stood up and excused himself to resume stretching.

"I think I'd like to be an electrician," Bobby vocalized for the first time. "I like the vibe. In my Uncle Ron's electrical business, when working with other electricians, it's all business. Handling electricity is dangerous! There's no room for horseplay. No picking on the fresh new guys."

"Yes," Jackie nodded. "That's why I love football. The teamwork. The camaraderie. When a football team wins, everybody wins, and we all celebrate together. Wrestling is such an individual sport…but it's basic in all of us. The first thing my brother and I ever did was wrestle. He was bigger and stronger, but sometimes he'd let me win."

"My older brother and I used to wrestle, too," Bobby remembered. "He wanted to be a plumber, so he would have fulfilled my dad's dreams. Now those aspirations have landed on my shoulders."

Jackie paused, thinking about his father and older brother. "One thing my older brother did for me was help me get out of serious trouble with my pops, especially this one time. We were wrestling in the basement, and I kicked the trophy case so hard one of the doors sprang open. Pops heard the rattling glass and rushed downstairs. Aaron took all the blame…saying that, as the older brother, he should have known better. I got in trouble, too…but not as bad as him. It created a bond between us."

"Dick and I had that bond, too," Bobby responded. "But now I'm left alone…Vietnam. My dad dreams of me being a plumber, and I don't know what to do."

"Sorry to hear about your brother," said Jackie. "Hearing you wrestle with your options makes me think about mine with football. About whether or not I should stay in Columbus after high school. My family could see me play if I catch on with the Buckeyes."

"And you'll make business contacts, too. My Uncle Ron stayed in Columbus after playing baseball for Ohio State, and his Rolodex is full of contacts from back then. Sometimes Columbus feels like a small town where everybody knows everybody else."

"Big decisions for both of us," Jackie mused. "Speaking of decisions, I'm glad you decided not to twist my knee off in the third period."

"And I bet you're glad I didn't bite you, either!"

Jackie suppressed a laugh as Bobby slowly shook his head.

"What got into that guy?" asked Jackie.

"I'm still trying to figure it out," said Bobby, shaking his head, "Nic's my practice partner, but that's one move he never practiced on me!"

Bobby began picking at a bit of plastic in the mat. "Nic hates to lose," Bobby said, "but if winning is all that matters…well, then, you can fool yourself into thinking that whatever you want to do is justified. You're free to do the devil's own work."

"I was taught the Golden Rule," said Jackie. "To think how your actions affect others, and if you'd want to be treated that way. Well, it *does* limit your options. I assume Nic wouldn't want anyone biting him!"

"Yeah, my Uncle Ron, the electrician, taught me the same thing," said Bobby, shaking his head as the image of a movie monster popped into his mind. "It's pretty clear that there wouldn't be a sport of wrestling if there was biting. I wouldn't want to wrestle Godzilla!"

"Me neither! How about Superman?" asked Jackie.

"I thought I was!" replied Bobby. "Near the end, when I was hopping on one foot near the scorer's table, I thought I was going to be launched over that table and into the stands!"

They both laughed at the imagined visual. "What stopped you?" asked Bobby.

"Witnesses!" joked Jackie. "No—well—in sports, I believe we can be competitors, not enemies. I want to beat you, not hurt you. Winning fair and square…that's what it's all about. I don't think those football coaches in the stands would accept anything less."

"Jackie…if you get that college scholarship, you'll get to use the college deferment. That, my friend, could be your ticket for avoiding the draft."

"Yes…as it stands right now. But I'm also praying for that high draft number."

"I could use a high number, too! College isn't an option for me. My dad thinks that everyone in college is a 'free-love, anti-war, dope-smokin' hippie.'"

Jackie rested his chin on his knees, looking hard at Bobby. "The question is…what do you want?"

"I know I want to stay out of Vietnam!" Bobby said, thinking about Dick. "But I feel like a grain of sand in an hourglass…sliding into the funnel with nothing to stop it. I can be drafted and sent to war, but I can't even vote. I'm not a conscientious objector…I don't know anyone in Canada…and the marriage exemption is long gone. So unless I get that high lottery number, I'll never be an electrician."

"I think you just said 'be an electrician,' Bobby!" said Jackie.

*I want to be an electrician,* Bobby realized. "But my dad thinks I'm so stupid that I'll electrocute myself."

"Tell your pops if a guy like me can go to college, then you can *certainly* be an electrician!"

"Oh my God! His head would explode!" said Bobby. Then he covered his mouth to block the words that had already escaped. He had just exposed his father's racism. But by the look on Jackie's face, Bobby knew this wasn't a surprise to the black wrestler from Columbus Clintonville.

Showing grace, Jackie ignored the comment about Bobby's father. "I guess I'm lucky I don't have your problem. I want to play football like my older brother, and my pops is okay with that," said Jackie.

"And I'm glad I don't have *your* problem," replied Bobby, catching Jackie's eye, "… not having a girlfriend!"

Jackie threw his head back and let go a single "Ha!" at the top of his lungs, enjoying the well-timed needle.

"A small win," said Bobby, also laughing, "but I'll take it!"

"So, Bobby, can you show me that 'duck-under' move?" Jackie asked.

"Well, Jackie, I might need to use it against you next year," Bobby said, realizing his desire to continue wrestling.

Bobby stood up, signaling his willingness. Soon, Jackie and Bobby were both in a tie-up, discussing the setup. When they were finished, Jackie said, "I'll work on that in practice and maybe use it next year."

"Not on me, right?" Bobby asked, feigning outrage.

"Don't worry, I'll never tie-up with you again, period." Jackie's words of respect lessened Bobby's pang from his defeat.

They shook hands, looking each other in the eye, wondering if their paths would ever cross again.

Bobby took off for the showers. Jackie took off, too.

# CHAPTER 20

★ ★ ★

## The Only Thing That Matters

.......................................................................

## Robert "Bobby" McCoy, Worthington Monroe 175-Pounder

**A**FTER HIS SHOWER, Bobby exited the locker room into a short hallway off the main one. His father was waiting for him.

"What's the matter with you?" Rick shouted, stopping Bobby dead in his tracks. "You were ahead of him, and you let him tackle you!" Poking a finger into Bobby's chest, Rick said with disgust, "I don't think you'll ever cut it."

"Dad, I tried—"

"No, you didn't. You had it in your hands, and you wouldn't put him away. You were ahead at the end! You could've protested when they took it away from you! But you didn't. And you're not even upset! In fact, when I came back into the gym, I saw you sitting with him…having a grand ole time. What's the matter with you?"

"Look, Dad, I – I – I didn't search him out! He came over to me…and s-started talking," Bobby stammered. "What was I *supposed* to do?"

"Get up and walk away!" Rick insisted, lowering his voice toward the end as nearby people started paying attention.

Rick used both fists to grab Bobby and push him against the wall. He stood nose-to-nose with his son.

"What could you *possibly* have in common with him?"

For a few seconds, Bobby said nothing, searching…and searching for an answer to please his father. But it was easier to just tell the truth.

"We have a *lot* in common," Bobby said, pushing back in an equal and opposite manner. Bobby had toughened up, indeed.

Bobby continued, "We both want a girlfriend. We both want to avoid Vietnam. And we both wanted to win a wrestling match… fair and square!"

Rick slowly released his grip and Bobby mirrored the action.

"Our union is full of guys like you," Rick said dismissively. "They won't vote to strike, but they'll take the increases when we win them. You had a chance in that last period to win…but you let go."

"Dad, you – you mean hurt him…*intentionally?*" asked Bobby.

"Well…injuries happen in football…in basketball…in all sports. Even in baseball! Players get hurt. It's part of the game. When a team wants to win, they take it to the other team and crush 'em."

Bobby stood still, standing ground. "I won't hurt someone on purpose. I'd rather lose than cheat. This isn't war, Dad. I want to play fair and square...by the rules, in wrestling and in life. That's what Uncle Ron teaches me. If I get a low lottery number and if I get drafted, I'll serve, just like you and Dick."

"I expect that! I'd expect you to serve! I wouldn't let you stay in my home if you wouldn't serve. I'd even block you from joining the union."

"I said I'd serve, Dad. *Please*...can't you at least be proud of me for that?"

Silence lay between them for a few seconds. Rick McCoy's nostrils flared as he breathed through his nose.

"And, about the union," Bobby continued, softly but assertively, "Jackie knew all about the guy who went around to the Columbus City high schools talking about entering the apprentice program if you passed the test."

"Yeah, so what? We'll win in court," Rick McCoy said, also standing ground, still nose to nose with his son.

Bobby paused and then made a decision. "Dad, I don't want that slot. I want to be an electrician. I want to work for Uncle Ron."

"*What?* You'll *never* make the money I make...and you'll never get a pension."

"But, Dad! I'll have steady work," Bobby argued. "That's what I'll need when I start out on my own!"

"You're too young and stupid to understand what I have. You'll wind up a loser just like Ron. Go work with him." Rick turned away from his son and took a couple of steps, then turned back and said, "On second thought, just go...go live with him." He waved his hand dismissively and walked away, turning left at the corner, searching for his wife.

"I will!" Bobby declared to the back of his father's head. Bobby followed but turned right in search of Cassie. As soon as he turned the corner, he spotted Cassie, and then his mom, standing by a nearby wall next to Gary's father, Carl Hamilton.

*They heard everything!* Bobby realized.

Spotting her husband walking away, Georgia looked at Bobby, and asked, "Could you get a ride home with Mr. Hamilton? My husband needs me." When Carl Hamilton shook his head yes, Georgia McCoy left to follow her husband.

Bobby grasped Cassie's hand and followed Carl Hamilton into the gym. The trio joined the Maverick gathering in the north stands in time for the beginning of the third round. It was a fun series of matches, two matches for each weight class. Each contestant, by virtue of making it to the third round, had already made districts...win or lose here. They wrestled aggressively with abandon...next-to-next-to-next. They threw moves they had never tried before in a match. Each battled and never gave up. Bobby smiled as he realized that this was the kind of match he had given Jackie. Gary, Gino, George, Jackie, and Lennie made the finals, but the Worthington Monroe Mavericks fell out of the team lead and into second place.

When the third round ended, the crowd began to dissipate. Coach Duke stood on the center mat, conferring with Assistant Coach Bennett while Lennie headed for the showers. Gary, now dressed in his street clothes after his shower, returned to the north stands and joined the trio.

"Nice cologne, Hambone...but did you have to marinate in it?" quipped Cassie.

"Need some more, buddy?" asked Bobby.

"Probably do," replied Gary. "What can I say? Julia loves this stuff!"

Coach Duke climbed noisily up the stands to command attention. "Okay, wrestlers, we'll be boarding the school bus as soon as Lennie gets back from the showers. Wait here...unless you have a ride home with your parents. The final round begins at 7:00 p.m. Doors open at 6:00 p.m. I'll be back here at 6:30 for those still wrestling. That's just over three hours from now."

Coach Duke excused those Mavericks whose parents could give them a ride home. Bobby watched Coach Duke step aside with Carl Hamilton and then turn their heads towards him. Catching Carl's eye, Bobby nodded when he was waved over. He grabbed Cassie's hand and led her into the conversation.

"Bobby and Cassie," said Carl, "Coach Duke gave me permission to take both of you home, if you'd like. But Bobby, if you want to ride the bus with your teammates, you can. Then, Gary and I will take Cassie home. What would you like to do, Cassie?"

"Well, I'd like to ride the school bus back with Bobby and the team, but I can tell that's not gonna happen!"

"You can bet your sweet bippy on that!" Carl quipped, doing his best imitation of Dick Martin from *Laugh-In*.

"Gary, I'm sorry, but I'm gonna have to miss your final, okay?" asked Bobby.

"I understand. No problem."

"Can I talk with you a minute, Cassie?" Bobby and Cassie stepped away. "Do you want to come with me to Uncle Ron's? I could walk you home from there."

Cassie agreed to the plan, and when they got to Carl's car, Gary took the front passenger seat as Bobby and Cassie climbed into the back. Carl Hamilton started the Lincoln Continental and used his electric window control to whirr down Gary's window. Looking at his son, he declared, "Whew! You reek!" He held his nose for effect.

Bobby and Cassie grinned at the good-natured needling, then reclined in their seats, taking their ease. As they drove off the Broadleaf school lot, Bobby asked, "Mr. Hamilton, what do you think will happen to Nic?"

"Well…let's think this through. He lost in the sectionals…so his season is over. And, he's a senior…so his high school wrestling career is over. They could ban him from spring sports, but I don't know if he plays one," Carl Hamilton reasoned. "But OHSIF will send a strong message that Nic's behavior will not be tolerated. His behavior threatens the very existence of the sport of wrestling. OSHIF will make sure it never happens again. And that might lead them to hand down penalties against next year's team, if team penalties are decided."

"They could penalize next years' wrestling program?" asked Gary.

"Team penalties, but nothing against Nic? That doesn't seem fair!" said Bobby.

"I'm not sure," Carl replied, "but I'll bet you that Coach Duke has found a dime and will be calling his athletic director. They'll both be reading the OHSIF rulebook tonight. They'll put up a defense. But Nic's bad decision could have a long-term impact."

*I hope I didn't make a bad decision today,* Bobby thought, taking short breaths. "Mr. Hamilton, why does everyone talk about winning being the only thing…when making a bad decision can have such negative consequences?"

"I see your point, Bobby," replied Carl. "Maybe we adults should start saying 'Making *good decisions* isn't everything…it's the only thing!'"

"The only thing that matters," agreed Cassie. "Looks like I made a good decision picking you." She playfully punched Bobby in the arm.

Bobby feigned a sore arm, rubbing it with his other. He paused, then said, "Mr. Hamilton, have you ever heard Billy Graham, or any other minister say anything about pursuing your own dreams versus your parents' plans? I know we're supposed to honor our parents, but…"

"That's an interesting question," replied Carl. "I'll have to think about that one."

"You might find the answer in the Gospel of John…John Phillips of the Mamas and the Papas, that is," quipped Gary, who then broke into song: "You gotta go where you wanna go, do what you wanna do, with whoever you wanna do it with…" [71]

Cassie dazzled as she took the lead, belting out: "You don't understand, that a girl like me can't love just one man…"

"Hey, Cassie, darling," Bobby interrupted, "Did you say '*CAN'T*' love just one man?"

"Oh, no – no! I said '*CAN*' sweetheart!" replied Cassie, recovering quickly. "You know I can only love you!"

Cassie had them all laughing. Amid the merriment, Gary looked over his shoulder and caught Bobby's eyes. They nodded, appreciating their mutual friendship and accepting the events of the day.

Gary looked away and reflected on how close he had come to losing his dream of making states. Like young Bouton, he had learned that the competition was fierce. Gary promised himself he would never take another opponent for granted.

Bobby turned and smiled at Cassie, who was still enjoying her own joke, sparkling in all the attention. Bobby accepted that his father's plans for him were no longer an option. Also, freed of his father's belief in winning at all costs, Bobby could now make his own decisions. His path forward led to Uncle Ron. A proud and assured smile broke across Bobby's face. When Cassie turned and they locked eyes, Bobby pictured her walking at his side, holding hands—his one and only.

★ ★ ★

**This quote is dedicated to all those who wrestle or put themselves in the field of play in any arena:**

"*IT IS NOT the critic who counts; not the man who points out how the strong man stumbles, or where the doer of deeds could have done them better.*

*The credit belongs to the man who is actually in the arena, whose face is marred by dust and sweat and blood; who strives valiantly; who errs, who comes short again and again, because there is no effort without error and shortcoming; but who does actually strive to do the deeds; who knows great enthusiasms, the great devotions; who spends himself in a worthy cause; who at the best knows in the end the triumph of high achievement, and who at the worst, if he fails, at least fails while daring greatly, so that his place shall never be with those cold and timid souls who neither know victory nor defeat.*"

—**Theodore Roosevelt,** April 23, 1910, The Sorbonne, Paris, France

**This drawing is dedicated to all
those who make states ...**

★ ★ ★ ★ ★ ★

★ ★ ★ ★ ★ ★

**... or equivalent in any sport or endeavor**

# ★ ★ ★ AFTERWORD ★ ★ ★

**D**URING THE 2020 elections, I heard news reporters and politicians claiming one candidate or the other was "tearing the social fabric of our nation." When I first heard the term "social fabric," I thought, *What is that?* Was it like the word "quality" which means different things to different people, such that it is really an empty word without context? For production engineers, the word "quality" means "adherence to a standard." So, for production engineers, the McDonald's hamburger is of the highest quality because it is the self-same product wherever you buy it. Not everyone agrees with that definition of quality.

So, what is the meaning of "social fabric"? Is there anything that unites us in America? What holds us all together? Is there a common thread that could be used to weave this social fabric? What can we all agree upon?

I believe it is The Golden Rule.

This is not a complex idea. We depend on The Golden Rule every day. If we drive our automobile past another motorist on a two-lane highway, we depend on them to stay in their right lane as they depend on us to stay in our right lane. Without belief in The Golden Rule, there would be no trust and traffic would need to slow to a crawl to pass each car. Life would be impossible.

The Golden Rule is the social fabric of human society.

## Here are some other ideals mentioned in the book:

*"I would prefer even to fail with honor than to win by cheating."*

**—Sophocles**

*"I disapprove of what you say, but I will defend to the death your right to say it."*

**—Attributed to Voltaire, but coined by author Evelyn Beatrice Hall in her book, *The Friends of Voltaire* (1906), to describe her subject's support of free speech.**[72]

However, when winning is all that matters, when the ends justify the means, then The Golden Rule is set aside…and chaos ensues. You saw a small example of this, in the book you just read, when Nic made the choice to injure another person in his quest to win at all costs.

Every major religion and philosophy on our planet has a version of The Golden Rule embedded in it. I noticed this a few years ago, when I went to the airport to pick up an arriving friend. I was early, so I waited in the Meditation Room. On the wall, there was a copy of The Golden Rule Poster.[73] It spelled out the concept in 13 different religions.

## I've included the chart below for reference. Here's an easy reading version:

- **Buddhism** – Treat not others in ways that you yourself would find hurtful.
- **Confucianism** – One word which sums up the basis of all good conduct … loving-kindness. Do not do to others what you do not want done to yourself.
- **Taoism** – Regard your neighbor's gain as your own gain, and your neighbor's loss as your own loss.
- **Sikhism** – I am a stranger to no one; and no one is a stranger to me. Indeed, I am a friend to all.
- **Christianity** – In everything, do to others as you would have them do to you; for this is the law and the prophets.
- **Unitarianism** – We affirm and promote respect for the interdependent web of all existence of which we are a part.
- **Native Spirituality** – We are as much alive as we keep the earth alive.
- **Zoroastrianism** – Do not do unto others whatever is injurious to yourself.

- **Jainism** – One should treat all creatures in the world as one would like to be treated.
- **Judaism** – What is hateful to you, do not do to your neighbor. This is the whole Torah; all the rest is commentary
- **Islam** – Not one of you truly believes until you wish for others what you wish for yourself.
- **Baha'i Faith** – Lay not on any soul a load that you would not wish to be laid upon you, and desire not for anyone the things you would not desire for yourself.
- **Hinduism** – This is the sum of duty; do not do to others what would cause pain if done to you.

Even many **Atheists** embrace The Golden Rule as a basis for morality and understanding empathy. Writing an op-ed in the Brainerd (Minnesota) Dispatch published on March 12, 2015, Amy LaValle Hansmann, founder of the Brainerd Area Atheists & Freethinkers, wrote: "If they wouldn't like someone hitting them with a stick, then why would they go around hitting someone else with one? It's not a terribly difficult concept to understand." [74]

The Golden Rule Poster on the following page was printed with the permission of Paul McKenna and the Interfaith Marketplace.

## Posters are available at:

https://www.interfaithmarketplace.com/home/ifm/page_130_24/golden_rule_poster.html

I hope this book has been an interesting read, and that it has inspired your interest in the sport of folkstyle wrestling. I hope it has provided an interesting snapshot of the historical and geographical setting – a time and place near and dear to my heart. And, I hope it has or will awaken a sense of purpose in you, that in your own time and place, you can make a difference in our nation and our world.

—*Dave Horning*

**HINDUISM**
This is the sum of duty;
do not do to others what would
cause pain if done to you
Mahabharata 5:1517

**BUDDHISM**
Treat not others in ways
that you yourself would
find hurtful
Udana-Varga 5.18

**BAHA'I FAITH**
Lay not on any soul a load
that you would not wish to
be laid upon you, and
desire not for
anyone the
things you
would not
desire for
yourself
*Baha'u'llah,*
*Gleanings*

**CONFUCIANISM**
One word which sums up the
basis of all good conduct...
loving kindness.
Do not do to
others what
you do not
want done
to yourself
*Confucius,*
*Analects 15.23*

**ISLAM**
Not one of you truly believes
until you wish for others what
you wish for yourself
*The Prophet Muhammad, Hadith*

**TAOISM**
Regard your neighbour's gain
as your own gain, and your
neighbour's loss as your own loss
*T'ai Shang Kan Ying P'ien, 213-218*

# THE GOLDEN RULE

**JUDAISM**
What is hateful to you,
do not do to your neighbour.
This is the whole Torah;
all the rest is commentary
*Hillel, Talmud, Shabbat 31a*

**SIKHISM**
I am a stranger to no one;
and no one is a stranger
to me. Indeed, I am
a friend to all
*Guru Granth Sahib, pg. 1299*

**JAINISM**
One should treat all
creatures in the world
as one would like
to be treated
*Mahavira, Sutrakritanga*

**CHRISTIANITY**
In everything, do to others
as you would have them
do to you; for this is the
law and the prophets
*Jesus, Matthew 7:12*

**ZOROASTRIANISM**
Do not do unto others
whatever is injurious
to yourself
*Shayast-na-Shayast 13.29*

**NATIVE SPIRITUALITY**
We are as much alive
as we keep the earth alive
*Chief Dan George*

**UNITARIANISM**
We affirm and promote respect
for the interdependent
web of all existence
of which we are a part
*Unitarian principle*

SCARBORO MISSIONS

A Christian Catholic community of priests and lay people
Designed by Kathy VanLoon
All rights reserved • Paul McKenna • 2000
To order poster, contact Brougham's, 2685 Danforth Ave., Toronto, Ontario, Canada, M4C 1L7
Tel (416) 690-6751 · Fax (416) 690-8267 Email: cplenglik@idirect.com

# ★ ACKNOWLEDGMENTS ★

To God, the creator of life

To Laura, my one and only

To Lauren, Alex, and Sam, for whom my love is unconditional

To all those who provided feedback and thereby helped me write this book, especially Amy, Bill, Bob, Ed, Gail, Garth, Gary, Karl, Kerry, Kathy, Laura, Marc, Mark, Merry, Mike, Patty, RC, Rick, Sharon, Teresa, and Tom, plus all the others who are too numerous to name individually but whose contributions mattered

To Bill, with appreciation for being such a great conversationalist

To Dennis, who believes that we should not argue, but instead, that we should discuss the issues of the day in an effort to better understand each other, that we should pursue clarity instead of agreement, that we can disagree without being disagreeable, and, instead of trying to win an argument, that we should try to discover "where is it exactly that we differ?"

To Glen, who preaches that all people, inclusive of persons of any nation, race, sexual orientation, gender identity and expression, political or philosophical outlook, or socio-economic status, are included in God's unconditional love and grace

To David, who is building a stronger, more inclusive community with a focus on developing a social infrastructure that unites the community for the common good

To Mark, whose drawings breathed life into what otherwise would have been tedious descriptions of wrestling, and who maintained a great and positive attitude throughout

To Limus, whose input helped make the dialog more realistic, and provided great friendship and entertainment throughout the process

To Arlyn, Kerry, and Cindy, my final copy editors, who provided a "Garfunkel touch" to the manuscript

To Kendra, whose formatting gave the book an artistic touch

To my cronies, who know me best and still befriend me

To all those who wrestle, because you are truly a person who, as described by Theodore Roosevelt..."is actually in the arena...who strives valiantly...who comes up short again and again...who knows great enthusiasms...and the triumph of high achievement"

To all who put themselves in the arena in any field of play. That alone doesn't make you a winner, but you will never be a winner if you don't.

# ★ ★ ★ ABOUT ★ ★ ★

## About the Author

Dave Horning is a graduate of Cornell University and the University of Chicago Graduate School of Business, where he studied under George Stigler, the winner of the Nobel Prize in Economics in 1982. Before the COVID pandemic of 2020, he worked in business valuation and helped small business owners find buyers for their businesses when they wanted to exit.

Dave is a member of the Ohio Business Brokers Association (OBBA) and has earned the Certified Valuation Analyst (CVA) designation from the National Association of Certified Valuators and Analysts (NACVA). He started writing his first book, *The Only Thing*, to stay productive during the pandemic. He was a member of the Westerville (Ohio) High School wrestling team for three years and the Cornell University wrestling team for one year. He is an avid golfer and skier.

For more information on all of Dave's endeavors, visit **www.davehorning.com**. He can also be reached via e-mail at: **theonlythingauthor@gmail.com**

## About the Illustrator

Mark Wilson studied at the Disney School of Animation taught by the Disney animators in Burbank, California. When computers became commonplace, Mark went to Platt College and studied graphic design and digital media. He worked for a publisher of children's books and is now a free-lance artist. Visit **www.markerdoodle.com**.

## About the Editor

Limus Woods is a professional writer/editor who has wrestled with words and sentences for much of his adult life. That's as close as he has ever gotten to wrestling, other than being a huge fan of the WWF growing up. You can find him on LinkedIn, or somewhere in Myrtle Beach reading near the ocean.

# ★ ★ ★ ENDNOTES ★ ★ ★

1        Wordhippo, "egalitarianism," *Wordhippo.com*, https://www.wordhippo.com/what-is/another-word-for/egalitarianism.html (accessed August 31, 2021).

2        The Balance, "Economic Statistics about 1971," *Thebalance.com*, https://www.thebalance.com /unemployment-rate-by-year-3305506 (accessed November 7, 2020).

3        Erik Sherman, "Inflation In 2021 is Nothing Like 1970s Inflation," *Forbes Magazine*, May 28, 2021, https://www.forbes.com/sites/eriksherman/2021/05/28/inflation-in-2021-is-nothing-like-1970s-inflation/?sh=4c925356ca0e (accessed June 4, 2021).

4        Trading investment, "100 Years Dow Jones Industrial Average Chart History (Updated)," *Tradingninvestment.com*, https://tradingninvestment.com/100-years-dow-jones-industrial-average-djia-events-history-chart/2/ (accessed May 18, 2020).

5        DollarTimes, "1971 Gas Price in Today's Dollars," *Dollartimes.com*, https://www.dollar items/price-of-a-gallon-of-gas-in-1971 (accessed May 18, 2020).

6        United States Census Bureau, "Facts about income wages, etc.," Census.gov, https://www. census .gov/library/publications/1972/demo/p60-85.html#:~:text=Median%20income %20of % 20the%20 the%20Nation%27s%20families%20went%20above,percent%20higher%20 than% 20the%201970%20median%20of%20%249%2C870 (accessed November 7, 2020).

7        DollarTimes, "1971 United States Minimum Wage in Today's Dollars," *Dollartimes. com*, https://www.dollartimes .com/inflation/items/1971-united-states-minimum-%2C%20 wage#:~:test=In%20the%20year%201971the,United%20States%20minimum%20wage%20 was%20%241.60 (accessed November 7, 2020).

7        United States Department of Labor, "History of Changes to the Minimum Wage Law," *Dol.gov*, https://www.dol.gov/agencies/whd/minimum-wage/history (accessed November 8, 2020).

8        Dermographia, "Metropolitan Area Median House Prices: 1971," *Demographia.com*, https:// demographia.com/db1971median.pdf#:~:text=Median%20House%20P%20i%20 %28i%201971%24%29%20Metropolitan%20Area,Charleston%20%2420%2C400%20Cincinnati%20%2417%2C500%20Cleveland%20%2428%2C700Cleveland%2428%2C700%20Columbus%20%2416%2C000 (accessed November 7, 2020).

9        Value Penguin, "Historical Mortgage Rates: Averages and Trends from the 1970s to 2020," *Valuepenguin.com,* https://www.valuepenguin.com/mortgages/historical-mortgage-rates#:~:text=In%201971%2C%20when%20Freddie%20Mac%20began%20surveying%20lenders,30-year%20fixed-rate%20mortgages%20ranged%20from%207.29%25%20to%207.73%25 (accessed November 7, 2020).

10       Andrew K. Dart, "The History of Postage Rates in the United States," Akdart.com, http://www.akdart.com/postrate.html (accessed November 7, 2020).

11       Billboard Magazine, "The Hot 100, Week of February 27, 1971," *Billboard.com,* https://www.billboard.com/charts/hot-100/1971-02-27 (accessed September 10, 2020).

12       Billboard Magazine, "Hot R&B/HipHop Songs," *Billboard.com,* https://www.billboard.com/charts/r-b-hip-hop-songs/1971-02-27 (accessed September 10, 2020).

13       Wikipedia, "Top-rated United States elevision programs of 1971-72," https://en.wikipedia. org/wiki/Toprated_United_States_television_programs_of_1971%E2%80%9372 (accessed September 10, 2020).

14       John Pearly Huffman and Car and Driver Magazine, "The 10 Best of 1970," *Caranddriver.com,* https://www.caranddriver.com/features/g30432994/the-10best-of-1970/ (accessed November 8, 2020).

15       Reader's Digest, "The Most Popular Car the Year You Were Born," *Rd.com,* https://www.rd.com/list/the-most-popular-car-the-year-you-were-born/ (accessed November 8, 2020).

16       Insider, "Here's what fast-food burgers cost every year," *Insider.com,* https://www.insider.com/fast-food-burgers-cost-every-year-2018-9#in-1971-your-burger-cost-an-average-of-030-6 (accessed November 8, 2020).

17       Doreen J. Uhas Sauer and Stuart Koblentz, *The Ohio State University Neighborhoods,* (Charleston SC: Arcadia Publishing, 2009).

18       Wikipedia, "Chic Harley," https://en.wikipedia.org/wiki/Chic_Harley, (accessed August 10, 2021).

19       Wikipedia, "Ohio Stadium," https://en.wikipedia.org/wiki/Ohio_Stadium, (accessed August 10, 2021).

20       Brent Greene and WOSU, "The Birth of Ohio Stadium," aired 1999 (Columbus: WOSU Columbus, 1999), Television.

21      The Ohio State University Athletic Department, "1968 Ohio State Football Roster," *Ohiostatebuckeyes.com,* https://ohiostatebuckeyes.com/wp-content/uploads/2018/07/1968 _Roster.pdf (accessed August 10, 2021).

22      1968-1970 Ohio State Buckeyes football team, *americanfootballdatabase.fandom.com,* https://americanfootballdatabase.fandom.com/wiki/1968_Ohio_State_Buckeyes_football_ team, https://americanfootballdatabase.fandom.com/wiki/1969_Ohio_State_Buckeyes_football_team, https://americanfootballdatabase.fandom.com/wiki/1970_Ohio_State_Buckeyes_ football_team (accessed August 10, 2021).

23      Stanford University Native American Cultural Center, "The Removal of the Indian Mascot of Stanford," *Nacc.standford.edu,* https://nacc.stanford.edu/about-nacc/history-time-lines/stanford-mascot-timeline/removal-indian-mascot-stanford (accessed November 8, 2020).

24      Sports Reference, "1973 Heisman Trophy Voting," *Sports-reference.com,* https://www. sports-reference.com/cfb/awards/heisman-1973.html (accessed August 10, 2021).

25      Suzanne Goldsmith, "'Lady wrestler' Looks Back on a Career in the Ring," *Columbus Monthly Magazine,* March 29, 2018,  https://www.columbusmonthly.com/news/20180329/lady-wrestler-looks-back-on-career-in-ring (accessed June 6, 2021).

26      Edmund Morris, Theodore Rex (New York: Random House, 2001).

27      Henry M. Littlefield, "The Wizard of Oz: Parable on Populism," *American Quarterly* 16, no. 1 (Spring 1964): 47-58.

27      Hugh Rockoff, "'The Wizard of Oz' as a Monetary Allegory," *Journal of Political Economy* 98, no. 4 (August 1990): 739-760.

28      Conrad C. Hinds, *The Great Columbus Experiment of 1908: Waterworks that Changed the World* (UK: The History Press, 2012).

29      Public Records Review, "Annexation Records," Publicrecordreviews.com, https:// www. publicrecordsreviews.com/annexation-records?gclid=CjwKCAjwqeWKBhBFEiwABo _XBh N66Xo6R6p94xVKFW2reI1_GzLhqKa1g06a_ARPuB1ycv_nEqxQ2RoCSiIQAvD_BwE (accessed February 18, 2020).

30      Wikipedia, "Worthington, Ohio." https://en.wikipedia.org/wiki/Worthington,_Ohio (accessed October 25, 2020).

31      The City of Columbus, "Annexations Overview," Columbus.gov, https://www.columbus.gov /planning/annexations/ (accessed February 18, 2020).

32      Columbus Public Schools, "Welcome to the Columbus City Schools Digital Dashboard – CCSD," *Columbuspublicschools.org,* https://ccsdashboard.eastus.cloudapp.azure.com/viewer/content/dashboard.html (accessed February 17, 2020).

33      New Albany-Plain Local Schools, "History of Win-Win Agreement," Napls.us, https://www. napls.us/Page/376 (accessed November 10, 2020).

34      Arnold Rampersad, *Jackie Robinson, A Biography* (New York: Ballantine Books, 1997).

35      Wikipedia, "1952 United States presidential election," https://en.wikipedia.org/wiki/1952 _United_States_presidential_election (accessed February 18, 2020).

36      Wikipedia, "1956 United States presidential election," https://en.wikipedia.org/wiki/1956 _United_States_presidential_election (accessed February 18, 2020).

37      Robert Siegel, Host, "When African American Voters Shifted Away From The GOP," NPR Radio, August 25, 2016, *Npr.org*, https://www.npr.org/2016/08/25/491389942/when-african-american-voters-shifted-away-from-the-gop (accessed August 12, 2020).

38      The author believes that the current state of racial divisiveness could have been obviated if President Eisenhower had more strongly supported the Modern Civil Rights movement of the 1950s. The author believes that the African American community of the 1950s was ready, willing, and able to embrace the capitalistic American economy were they given equal opportunity which President Eisenhower could have championed. The author was inspired to this idea by a play presented at the Vern Riffe Theatre in Columbus Ohio about then Vice-President Nixon, titled "*That's My Boy!*" The author was unable to locate references for the play or its playwright. The author welcomes assistance in providing the proper attribution.

39      Wikipedia, "1968 Olympics Black Power salute," https://en.wikipedia.org/wiki/1968_Olympics_Black_Power_salute#:~:text=During%20their%20medal%20ceremony%20in%20the%20Olympic%20Stadium,US%20national%20anthem%2C%20%22%20The%20Star-Spangled%20Banner%20%22 (accessed November 7, 2020).

40      Tom Schad, "Olympian John Carlos on 1968 Brent Musbarger Criticism: He 'Doesn't Even Exist in My Mind,'" USA Today (Tysons, Virginia), May 30, 2019, Sports 1.

41      The Ohio State University Athletic Department, "Bill Willis," *Ohiostatebuckeyes.com,* https://ohiostatebuckeyes.com/bill-willis/ (accessed August 10, 2021).

42      National Football League Hall of Fame, "Bill Willis," *Profootballhof.com,* https://www.profootballhof.com/players/bill-willis/ (accessed August 10, 2021).

43      Zach Meisel, "Football, racism and an unbreakable bond: The tale of Rudy Hubbard and Woody Hayes," *Cleveland.com,* January 12, 2019, https://www.cleveland.com/ osu/2013 /09/ football_ racism_and_an_unbreak.html (accessed August 10, 2021).

44      Glenn Sattell, "The Historic Alabama-USC 1970 Matchup That Changed Football in the South," *Saturdaydownsouth.com,* 2016, https://www.saturdaydownsouth.com/alabama-football/ historic-alabama-usc-matchup-1970/ (accessed August 12, 2021).

45      Steven Travers, *One Night, Two Teams: Alabama vs. USC and the Game That Changed a Nation* (Lanham MD: Taylor Trade Publishing, 2007).

46      Desmond Wilcox, "The Americans, The Football Coach, Ohio State Football Woody Hayes," *Youtube.com,* June 29, 2011,  https://www.youtube.com/watch?v=AZCnocVvhgA (accessed September 22, 2021).

46      Desmond Wilcox, *"The Football Coach,"* The Americans, season 1, episode 13, aired April 10, 1978 (London: BBC, 1978), Television.

46      Desmond Wilcox, *Americans* (New York: Delacorte Press, 1978).

47      Richard Schneirov, *Pride and Solidarity: A History of the Plumbers and Pipefitters of Columbus, Ohio, 1889-1989* (Ithaca NY: Cornell University ILR Press, 1993), 105, 107.

48      Wikipedia, "Black History Month," https://en.wikipedia.org/wiki/Black_History_Month#:~:text=Black%20History%20Month%20was%20first%20proposed%20by%20black,later%2C%20from%20January%202%20to%20February%2028%2C%201970 (accessed November 5, 2020).

49      Editors, "School Principals Seek End to Student Clashes," *Columbus Evening Dispatch* (Columbus, Ohio), February 22, 1971, 10A.

50      Wikipedia, "Angela Davis," https://en.wikipedia.org/wiki/Angela_Davis (accessed November 5, 2020).

51      LaQuita Henry, "LaQuita Henry '71," *Ohio State Alumni Magazine,* Fall 2018, 52.

52      John Sidney Evans, "John Sidney Evans '70," *Ohio State Alumni Magazine,* Fall 2018,

53      Jay Shaffer, "Jay Shaffer'69," *Ohio State Alumni Magazine,* Fall 2018, 59.

54      Editors, "Year End Review of 1971 Columbus," *Call and Post* (Columbus, Ohio), January 1, 1972, 2B-5B.

55      The Corporation: Berry Gordy, Alphonso Mizell, Frederick Perren and Deke Richards, "Mama's Pearl." Motown, The Jackson 5 Third Album, 1970, *AZLyrics.com*, https://www.azlyrics.com/lyrics/jackson5/mamaspearl.html (accessed July 20, 2021).

56      Sports Reference, "1952 World Series Game 1, Yankees at Dodgers, October 1," *Baseball-reference.com,* https://www.baseball-reference.com/boxes/BRO/BRO195210010.shtml (acessed October 29, 2020).

57      Joe Posnanski, *The Soul of Baseball: A Road Trip Through Buck O'Neil's America* (New York: HarperCollins, 2008).

58      Military Factory, "Vietnam War Casualties (1955-1975)," *Militaryfactory.com*, https://www.militaryfactory.com/vietnam/casualties.asp (accessed November 8, 2020).

59      Wikipedia, "Vietnamization," https://en.wikipedia.org/wiki/Vietnamization (accessed November 11, 2020).

60      Robert D. Sander, *Invasion of Laos, 1971: Lam Son 719* (Norman OK: University of Oklahoma Press, 2014).

61      AP, "S. Viet Base in Laos Overrun," *Columbus Citizen-Journal* (Columbus, Ohio), February 26, 1971, 1.

62      Peter Shapiro, "Freshman Deferments End As Nixon Signs New Draft Legislation," *Harvard Crimson* (Cambridge, Massachusetts), September 29, 1971, https://www.thecrimson.com/article/1971/9/29/freshman-deferments-end-as-nixon-signs/.

63      Wikipedia, "Paris Peace Accords," https://en.wikipedia.org/wiki/Paris_Peace_Accords (accessed November 8, 2020).

64      The Nixon Center, "The Paris Agreement on Vietnam: Twenty-Five Years Later," *Mtholyoke.edu,* https://www.mtholyoke.edu/acad/intrel/paris.htm (accessed November 8, 2020).

65      George Jackson, "One Bad Apple." MGM, Osmonds, 1970, *Songlyrics.com*, http://www.songlyrics. com/the-osmonds/one-bad-apple-lyrics/ (accessed July 20, 2021)

66      Wikipedia, "Swann v. Charlotte-Mechlenberg Board of Education," https://en.wikipedia.org/ wiki/Swann_v._Charlotte-Mecklenburg_Board_of_Education

67      Jim Bouton, *Ball Four* (New York: World Publishing, 1970).

68      Jerry Kramer and Dick Schaap, *Instant Replay: The Green Bay Diary of Jerry Kramer* (New York: Anchor Books, 1968).

69      Wil Haygood, *Tigerland •1968-1969 •A City Divided, a Nation Torn Apart, and a Magical Season of Healing* (New York: Alfred A. Knopf, 2018).

70      Wikipedia, "Gorgeous George," https://en.wikipedia.org/wiki/Gorgeous_George (accessed May 18, 2021).

71      John Phillips, "Go Where You Wanna Go," Dunhill Records, If You Can Believe Your Ears and Eyes, 1965, *AZLyrics.com,* www.azlyrics.com/lyrics/mamasandthepapas/gowhereyouwanna go.html (accessed July 2, 2021).

72      S. G. Tallentyre, S.G. (1906). *"Helvetius: The Contradiction". The Friends of Voltaire* (London: Smith, Elder, & Co, 1906), 199.

73      Interfaith Marketplace, "The Golden Rule Poster," *Interfaithmarketplace.com,* https://www.interfaithmarketplace.com/home/ifm/page_130_24/golden_rule_poster.html (accessed October 29, 2020).

74      Amy LaValle Hansmann, "An Atheist View of the Golden Rule," *Brainerd Dispatch* (Brainerd, Minnesota), March 12, 2015, https://www.brainerddispatch.com/opinion/columns/3698993-guest-opinion-atheist-view-golden-rule.

# RECOMENDED READING ★ ★ ★

★ ★ ★

1. Wil Haygood, *Tigerland • 1968-1969 • A City Divided, a Nation Torn Apart, and a Magical Season of Healing* (New York: Alfred A. Knopf, 2018).

2. Steven Travers, *One Night, Two Teams: Alabama vs. USC and the Game That Changed a Nation* (Lanham MD: Taylor Trade Publishing, 2007).

3. Jerry Kramer and Dick Schaap, *Instant Replay: The Green Bay Diary of Jerry Kramer* (New York: Anchor Books, 1968).

4. Arnold Rampersad, *Jackie Robinson, A Biography* (New York: Ballantine Books, 1997).

5. Joe Posnanski, *The Soul of Baseball: A Road Trip Through Buck O'Neil's America* (New York: HarperCollins, 2008).

6. Richard Schneirov, *Pride and Solidarity: A History of the Plumbers and Pipefitters of Columbus, Ohio, 1889-1989* (Ithaca NY: Cornell University ILR Press, 1993), 105, 107.

7. John Grisham, *Playing for Pizza* (New York: Dell, 2007).

8. Desmond Wilcox, *Americans* (New York: Delacorte Press, 1978).

9. Daniel James Brown, *The Boys in the Boat: Nine Americans and Their Epic Quest for Gold at the 1936 Berlin Olympics* (New York: Penguin Books, 2013).

10. Edward Dolan and Richard Lyttle, *Archie Griffin* (New York: Pocket Books, 1977).

11. Archie Griffin with Dave Diles, *Archie: The Archie Griffin Story* (Garden City NY: Doubleday & Company, 1977).

12. Maxwell Maltz, *Psycho-Cybernetics* (New York: Simon & Schuster, 1960).

13. Joe Weasel, *The Lost College Basketball Legacy of Fred Taylor* (Wilmington OH, Orange Frazer Press, 2002).

14. AAREG (aka African American Registry), "Black History in the Vietnam War, a Brief Story," *Aaregistry.org*, https://aaregistry.org/story/black-history-in-the-vietnam -war-a-brief-story/ (accessed November 8, 2020).

15. The American War Library, "Vietnam War Casualties by Race, Ethnicity and Natl Origin," *Americanwarlibrary.com*, https://www.americanwarlibrary.com (accessed November 8, 2020).

16. Chris Fowler, Host, "ESPN Classic Sports Century: Dan Gable Documentary," *Youtube.com*, 2010, https://www.youtube.com/watch?v=r4tGup3FnIs (accessed August 7, 2021).

17. Institute of the Black World, "Black Reflections On 1971," *Call and Post* (Columbus, Ohio), January 1, 1972, 1B.

18. Wikipedia, "1973 oil crisis," https://en.wikipedia.org/wiki/1973_oil_crisis (accessed November 7, 2020).

# BOOK CLUB QUESTIONS

★ ★ ★    ★ ★ ★

1. Do you think that winning is everything? Have you ever been part of an organization or activity that took this too far?

2. Do you believe in the Golden Rule? Do you believe it is the "social fabric" that holds us together? Why or why not?

3. Do you estimate that almost everyone knows about the Golden Rule? What percentage of our society do you believe thinks about the Golden Rule before acting or making a decision?

4. Who was your favorite character and why? Which character did you like the least and why?

5. Did you enjoy the historical interludes? Was there an interesting fact that caught your attention?

6. Have you ever been wronged by a person and then tried to explain the Golden Rule to them? Did you have any luck?

7. What was the best decision you ever made? What was the worst?

8. Did you enjoy learning about folkstyle wrestling? Will you attend a middle school, high school or collegiate wrestling match in the next year?

9. Have you ever enjoyed a conversation with a person whose background was different than yours?

# An Overview of the Rules of Folkstyle Wrestling in 1970-71

There are many different forms of wrestling, from Olympic ("Freestyle" and "Greco-Roman") to Professional Wrestling. The wrestling in American high schools and colleges is called "Folkstyle" or "Collegiate" wrestling.

**Please note that, over time, the rules of wrestling have changed, but as of February, 1971, the rules in Ohio for high school wrestling were basically as follows:**

- Each match is divided into three (3) periods, each two (2) minutes long.

- Before the start of the match, one wrestler is designated to wear a green ankle band, and the other is designated to wear a red ankle band. In this book, the Worthington Monroe Maverick wrestlers wear green uniforms, always wear the green ankle band and always have their score listed first. Therefore, a score of "3-6" would mean that the Worthington Monroe Maverick wrestler, the Green wrestler, was losing to the Red wrestler by the score of 3 to 6. The Red wrestler would be winning by the score of 3-6.

- Before the start of the match, the Referee instructs the Green and Red wrestlers to shake hands. Both wrestlers start the First Period from the **Neutral Position**; that is, both wrestlers are standing up on their feet looking at each other across the center of the mat.

This is what the **Neutral Position** looks like:

- At the end of the first period, the Referee flips a coin or a disc. The winner of the "coin toss" selects whether they want to start the second period on top or on bottom. They switch positions for the third period (the final period).

- At the start of the second and third Periods, the wrestlers start from what is called the **Referee's Position.**

This is the **Referee's Position:**

The wrestler on the bottom (who has both hands on the mat) is referred to as being in the **"Down Referee's Position"** ("Down Position"). This wrestler is also called the **Defensive Wrestler** because they are trying to avoid being pinned. Their opponent is in the **"Top Referee's Position"** ("Up Position" or "Top Position" or "Control Position") and is called the **Offensive Wrestler.**

- If the wrestlers are evenly matched, then the Offensive Wrestler will have difficulty pinning their opponent. Ironically, the Defensive Wrestler will thus have a better chance of generating points, via an **Escape** or **Reversal** (see below).

## At a wrestling match or tournament, there are two types of scoring:

1. **INDIVIDUAL POINTS:** the points that a wrestler earns during a match for successfully completing certain types of moves, and

2. **TEAM POINTS:** the points that a team earns as a result of their individual wrestler's victory.

- A wrestling match can be won by outscoring the opponent (winning by a "**Decision**") or by pinning the opponent (winning by a "**Fall**"). Even though a wrestler may be far behind, that wrestler can achieve sudden victory by pinning their opponent. The match is over when one wrestler pins the other.

## In 1971, an individual wrestler could earn individual points during a match by successfully completing the following types of moves:

- **TAKEDOWN – Two (2) Points:** taking an opponent from the Neutral Position to the mat and gaining control.

- **ESCAPE – One (1) Point:** when a Defensive Wrestler gains a Neutral Position.

- **REVERSAL – Two (2) Points:** when a Defensive Wrestler switches places with his opponent and becomes the Offensive Wrestler.

- **PENALTY POINTS** – for Stalling, Dangerous Holds, and other inappropriate activities. The referee will first issue a warning, which results in no points, but subsequent infractions will incur a one point penalty, then another one point penalty, then a two-point penalty, and then disqualification.

- **BACK POINTS**

  - **PREDICAMENT (aka "Near Fall 2", today) – Two (2) Points:** when the Offensive Wrestler briefly puts the Defensive Wrestler on his back or comes within a 45-degree angle of doing so.

  - **NEAR FALL (aka "Near Fall 3", today) – Three (3) Points:** like a Predicament, but the Defensive Wrestler is very close to getting pinned and the pinning move is held for at least five seconds.

- **FALL (aka "PIN") – Instant Victory!** When the Offensive Wrestler holds both Defensive Wrestler's shoulders to the mat for two full seconds. No points are awarded … the match is over.

- **RIDING TIME – Zero (0), One (1) or Two (2) Points:** Riding Time points are awarded at the end of the match. A wrestler earns one (1) riding time point if they are in the Up Referee's Position and thus in control of their opponent for a period of time that exceeds the time they were in the Down Referee's Position by more than a minute. Two points (maximum) if more than two (2) minutes.

  *Examples:*

  - *Green earns 2:30 riding time; Red earns 1:45 riding time; Neutral Position 1:45 ---- > no points*

  - *Green earns 2:30 riding time; Red earns 1:15 riding time; Neutral Position 2:15 ---- > 1 point Green*

  - *Green earns 1:15 riding time; Red earns 3:30 riding time; Neutral Position 1:15 ---- > 2 points Red*

  ***These rules were in effect in February 1971.***


- **Interesting Pointers and Strategies:** Wrestling is a contact sport that tests body and mind. Contestants are matched according to weight, enabling each person of a certain size to compete in their own class. Wrestling has special appeal because there is constant motion, and each wrestler executes their own creative variation of common moves, sometimes inventing their own! Strength is important, but speed, flexibility, balance, endurance, and execution are equally important. The individual character of wrestling makes each victory or defeat a personal responsibility; privilege provides no advantage.

- **Tournament Brackets:** The bracket below is a sample bracket which explains seeding and many other unique terms associated with the 16 Sectional Tournaments taking place all over Ohio on Saturday, February 27. 1971. These were all "single elimination" tournaments. There were no "wrestlebacks," which afford a second opportunity for those who lose in the first or second round to still have a chance to reach the semi-final, and thus advance to the districts. Any wrestler who lost in the first two rounds was eliminated from the tournament; their season was over.

The purpose of seeding is to keep the best wrestlers away from each other until the later rounds.

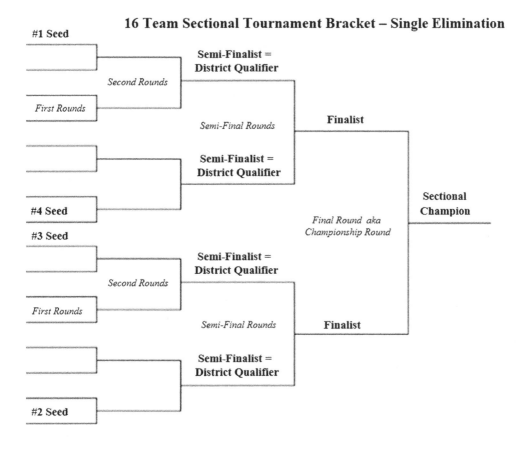

**16 Team Sectional Tournament Bracket – Single Elimination**

*NOTE: In 1971, the top four in the sectionals make districts. The top two in the districts make states.*

Made in the USA
Monee, IL
06 December 2021

84091667R00149